Slivers of Peace

His Warriors

Book 3

By

Ronna M. Bacon

Verses

Isaiah 57:18-19 I have seen what they do, but I will heal them anyway! I will lead them. I will comfort those who mourn, bringing words of praise to their lips. May they have abundant peace, both near and far,' says the Lord, who heals them.

John 14:27. Peace I leave with you; my peace I give you. I do not give to you as the world gives. Do not let your hearts be troubled and do not be afraid.
(NKJV)

Table of Contents

Prologue

He watched from the shadows as the young girl scurried down the forest path, tripping as she watched behind her. She had heard something there and she was scared. She had been told not to come out there, but the forest drew her. She needed to be there, to draw her maps and pictures.

She knew better. The sun was getting low and her parents would not be happy with her. She tripped, her hands flying out to break her fall, her backpack banging against her. She lay for a minute, catching her breath, before rising and brushing herself off.

She heard the low laugh behind her and spun, fear on her face, trying to find the man she knew was there. She couldn't see him. She flew down the path towards her bike, needing to get away. What if he caught her? What would he do with her?

The man followed more slowly, satisfied that he had scared her away. He watched as she pedaled as hard as she could to escape. He knew who she was and where to find her. He turned back to the path and then stopped. No, today was not the day. He had many hours and days of planning. He could wait for the right time, no matter how long it took.

Chapter 1

*H*is face upraised to the sun, Ezekiel Williams stood leaning against his truck, arms extended onto the hood. He could feel the change in the air. A storm was moving in, he was sure, and he wanted to be ready to follow it, if possible. His hazel eyes popped open and he turned to look around. There it was again. That feeling he was followed and watched. Who and why, he had no idea. He didn't make any enemies. He ran a hand through his auburn hair, messing it up more than he already had, and sighed, turning towards the building he was parked in front of. Delaying it wouldn't change the situation, he thought. He needed to speak with the cartographer today, to see if his maps were accurate for the area he was planning on studying. He pulled the paper from his shirt pocket. P. Matthews, Cartographer, it read. He was told that this person was one of the best in the business, that the maps they provided were accurate.

He paced through the gravel parking lot, dust kicking up from his runners. The area was so dry, he thought. We need rain, but I would love a good thunderstorm to watch. Pushing open the door, he entered the office, looking around for someone he could talk to. He had made an appointment and the female who answered had told him P. Matthews would be in the office that day.

A sudden yell from the back had him jumping, then heading back through the office. A running figure hit him head on and sent both of them flying, the man picking himself up and sending a kick at Zeke for being in his way. Zeke curled into a ball, arms folding around his abdomen, at the pain. His vision blurred, then cleared. He lay still for a minute, then gingerly picking himself up, headed towards the rear of the building.

"Hello? Anyone back here?" He hesitated to enter what he knew would be the office area but felt he had no choice. He searched for the person who had called, certain it was a woman.

Finally, in the last office he came to, he found her, on her side, her arms wrapped protectively around her head. He stooped to check on her, then pulled out his phone to call for the emergency services he knew was needed. Lord, let her be okay, please? I can't take anyone else being hurt because of me. Zeke's mind traveled back in time and he lost the sense of where he was.

Hearing a sound from the front of the office, he paced back that way, grimacing at the pain he felt. A younger woman stared at him.

"What are you doing back there?" She set the parcels she was holding on the front desk. "Where's Paige?"

"Paige?"   Zeke was puzzled and turned to stare behind him. "Paige? As in the last office?"

She nodded. "Paige. What did you do to her?" She brushed to go by him.

"She's been hurt. I walked in on it."

The woman, girl actually, spun to stare at him, then almost ran for the back. He could hear her calling for Paige as he heard the sirens cut off and officers walk through the door.

"Zeke?" He turned as he heard a voice and saw a friend.

"Jason? Your patrol area?"

Jason Long nodded, then studied the man standing in front of him. "What happened, Zeke?"

"First, there's a woman back there that needs paramedics. She was being assaulted when I walked in."

Jason nodded, then pointed towards a chair in the reception area. "Sit. I'll be back in a few minutes. We need someone to look at you as well."

Zeke just shook his head as Jason walked away, then found a seat. This was not how he was planning on spending his day. Who was that man anyway? He could hear quiet voices from the back. One of the paramedics walked towards him.

"Jason says you were hit. Let me check you out."

Zeke shook his head. "I'm fine. Just a few bruises."

The paramedic shook his head. "Doesn't work that way. Jason won't let you leave until I do."

Zeke sighed, then submitted to the examination. Pulling his T-shirt back down, he stared past the paramedic towards the hallway.

"How is she?"

"Paige? She's on her feet, madder than all get out. She's trying to figure out how the man got in and what he wanted."

Zeke nodded as he stood and headed back that way.

"Hey, wait! I don't think you're supposed to be back there." The paramedic followed in his wake.

Zeke shrugged. "Doesn't matter. I'm going back there any way." He stopped and watched as the woman he had found on the floor, Paige he thought he remembered her name was, shrugged off the paramedic. He smiled.

"Zeke? Tell me what you saw." Jason stood in front of him, blocking his line of sight.

"Other than a huge man in camouflage coming at me? Nothing but stars and I don't mean the ones I enjoy watching."

Jason smothered his grin and shook his head. "Nothing stands out?"

Zeke shook his head. "Is she okay?"

Jason angled his body so he could watch Paige. "She says she is and like you is refusing to go to Emerge. Now, anything at all, Zeke?"

Zeke shook his head, watching as Paige walked towards him, her gray eyes shadowed and her cap of short red-gold curls tousled. "Not that I can think of. It just happened so fast."

Jason nodded, then turned back to Paige. "Paige?"

She just stared at him until he smiled.

"I know. You've told me everything you can remember. But if any else comes up, call me. You too, Zeke." Jason walked away, the two left behind staring at him.

Zeke turned to the woman, around his own age he thought, and held out his hand.

"I'm Ezekiel Williams, Zeke to my friends."

Paige stared at him, then down at his hand, finally sighing as she shook it. "I'm

Paige Williams.   I believe we had an appointment for this afternoon, but it doesn't look as if we'll be keeping it." She turned abruptly and paced to the front of the building.   "Meg, flip the phones over to voice mail and head on home. Better yet, here." She dug into her pocket, pulling out some money.   "Gerry's off today, isn't he? Take this. Get all prettied up and have him take you to the Italiano for dinner. You two don't get out for meals very often."   She turned to stare behind her.   "We won't be working anymore today."

"Are you sure, Paige?" Meg stared at her boss. "I can stay."

Paige shook her head. "No point both of us wasting our day watching time tick by. Go.   Enjoy the day with Gerry.   And thanks." She watched as Meg walked away, then turned back to Zeke.   "Now, I understand you were specific as to maps you wanted to see?"

He nodded, then looked back down the hallway.   "I am, but it doesn't look as if we'll be able to look at them, does it?"

She sighed again. "No, it doesn't. I was working in the one office, heard a noise and knew I was alone in the office. I walked in on him tossing the back office where I keep the older maps." She frowned. "Now, why would he want them?"

Zeke shrugged. "I have no idea but it looks as if your coffee's getting cold." He pointed at Meg's desk.

She nodded. "It is. I had Meg pick up one for you as well."

Chapter 2

*P*aige stood in her office doorway the next morning, looking around. What had that man wanted yesterday? She didn't keep anything in the office that anyone wanted. Just old maps and maps she was currently working on. She sighed, then headed for the back office, knowing she had a full morning's work ahead of her and Meg to sort through all the maps and put them back in order, to say nothing of the cleaning they needed to do. Zeke had asked if he could return that afternoon, and Paige had not had the heart to refuse him, even though she had planned to take the afternoon off and just wander through the forest. Maybe that wasn't such a good idea anymore, she thought. Jason hadn't been able to tell her who the man was. There just wasn't the evidence to name him. She remembered the gloves on his hands and raised her own hand to her face. The bruise on her cheek was

16

now deep purple and sore, even with icing it last night.

Lord, I don't feel safe anymore here in town. Why not? I've been running from town to town for so long, I need to stop. I need to find that peace again that I used to have.

She turned as she heard the front door open and then silence. Heart in her throat, she edged towards the front of the office.

"Meg? Is that you?"

"It's Zeke, Paige. I didn't mean to startle you." He watched with concern the panic in her eyes as she appeared in the hallway.

"Zeke? What are you doing here? It's not afternoon, yet. At least, I don't think it is." She stared at him, her eyes blurring from lack of sleep.

Zeke studied the woman in front of him, noting the dark circles under her eyes. "How's the face today?" He nodded at the bruise.

"Sore. How would you expect it to feel?" She was grumpy and knew it. "I'm sorry. I shouldn't bite at clients."

Zeke shrugged. "It's not a problem. Now, what can I do to help you? Unless a thunderstorm comes up, I'm free for the day."

She turned and looked behind her, sighing. "Thank you, Zeke. It's such a mess. Oh, there's Meg."

Zeke turned to greet Meg, finding her somewhat hostile.

"What are you doing here? You're not supposed to be here until this afternoon."

"Meg! That's enough!" Paige's voice cut through Meg's anger. "He didn't have anything to do with what happened."

"And how do you know that?" Meg turned towards Paige, her anger still flaring.

"Because I do. It's not for you to question. Now, let's get to work. Meg, can you clear off the big table? We're going to need that. I'll start coffee and then we can get to work. Come on, Zeke. Let me give you a tour."

Meg glared after him, worry for Paige utmost in her mind. Then she sighed. Yes, her sister knew exactly what she was doing and she needed to trust her. Paige would tell

Meg that God had her back and He was in control.

Paige straightened up and rubbed her back three hours later. With Zeke's help, they had managed to sort all the maps and file them again. It had been a long morning, though. She turned to find Zeke watching her, a thoughtful look in his eyes.

"Zeke?"

Zeke gave himself a mental shake. "Paige? Let me take you two ladies to lunch. Then we can come back and take a look at those maps I would like to see."

Paige shook her head. "That's not necessary."

Zeke grinned at her, dimples appearing. "It is. It's not often I have the privilege of escorting two lovely ladies for lunch."

"Just say yes, Paige. I'm starving." Meg appeared behind Zeke, a question on her face her sister didn't want to answer.

Paige sighed. "All right, then. Let's go. Where to?"

"Somewhere off the beaten track, perhaps. I found a nice little cafe not far from here that's a hidden gem."

Seated across from Zeke in the small diner he had taken them too, Paige studied the menu, then the man across from her who was talking with her sister. He had managed to win Meg over during the morning. She listened to their conversation, then lifted her eyes. She knew someone was there who meant her harm. Who was it? She searched the diner, her eyes stopping on the few diners in there, then dropping back to her plate as her order was set in front of her.

"How did you ever manage to find this place, Zeke? You're not from here. We are and I didn't know it existed." Meg bit into a French fry, watching Zeke as he looked at her.

"Jason."

"Jason?" Paige spoke up.

"Jason Long, the officer who responded yesterday. He's become a good friend of mine. His sister married one of my best friends."

Paige nodded, but didn't pursue the topic any further. She really didn't like being on the police radar for any reason. There was too much garbage in her past to have that happen.

Zeke pulled out his phone as it chimed, noting the alert he had received, a smile on his face.

"That looks like good news." Meg was fishing and they all knew it.

"Meg! It's none of your business."

She shrugged, an unrepentant grin on her face. She had reached the point with Zeke that they were both teasing each other like siblings.

"It's okay, Paige." Zeke frowned a little at the look on her face. "It's just an alert that a storm is moving in. It's to hit tonight, which means no sleep for me."

"You stay up and watch the storms? Cool." Meg had found a new interest, Paige thought.

Back in the office, Paige took a minute by herself, not quite sure what she was feeling. Yesterday had stirred up too much for her and she hadn't been able to process it all yet.   She turned as she heard quiet footsteps stop behind her.

"Are you okay, Paige?"   Zeke was concerned, seeing the shadows in her eyes.

"I will be. It's just…." Her voice died away and she started to brush by him, stopping as he laid a hand on her arm.

"Don't hide your feelings from me, Paige.   I consider you a friend now and would like to help."

She snorted. "Like you can find this guy and figure out why?"

Zeke tilted his head, studying the bruise on her face, feeling that it wasn't the first time she had faced something like this. "No, I can't, but I would like to be your friend. Friends care about one another. Just know that I'm praying for you."

She turned her eyes on him, disbelief flickering through them. "Well, the way I see it, God could have stopped this before it happened, not let it happen." She walked away from him, heading for the room with the maps in it.

Zeke sighed, then turned to follow her, finding Meg standing beside him.   He studied the young woman, noting the shadows in the eyes.

"Meg?" His voice was barely above a whisper.

She shook her head. "She's hurting, Zeke, and I have no idea why. It's been like that for years. She just came back home about four years ago and set up her business. Before that, she wandered all over. Mom and Dad are worried about her." Her voice was equally low. "She'll deny it if you ask her, but I find her up at night, just sitting and staring into nothing." She turned worried eyes to Zeke. "What can I do to help her?"

"Prayer, Meg. Pray for your sister." He nodded towards the office Paige had disappeared in. "I'm planning on sticking around, too. Something's going on."

Meg snorted. "Ya think? She won't say anything, though. That's Paige."

Zeke nodded, hesitated and headed back to where Paige was laying out maps.

Chapter 3

Zeke laid his file on the table, then turned to Paige. He was worried about her but didn't know her well enough to know how to approach it.

She glared at him, then pointed at the maps. "Here are the maps you wanted to see. Why?"

Zeke sighed to himself, then pulled out a sheet of paper from the folder. "Just some background. I'm a freelance meteorologist. I make a study of an area to see the weather patterns and their effect on the earth. This area has me stumped." He handed her the paper. "What I saw from the air is different from other maps I've looked at. It doesn't look like a natural disturbance."

Paige shot him a quick look and then taking the paper, laid it down on the map, her fingers tracing the area. "This map is the one I did about two years ago. This is just recent?" She looked up at him as he stood beside her, and he nodded. "There is a definite difference." She paused again, chewing at her lower lip.

Then she turned. "Meg? What's the schedule like for the next couple of days?"

"No clients, Paige." She appeared at the doorway. "You're going on a field trip?"

"I might need to. And you want to come?"

Meg grinned at her. "I do."

Paige stared at her sister, not sure if she wanted her to be involved in this. Her instincts were telling her to run from this as far and as fast as she could, but the man standing beside her changed that on her. For once, maybe she could face what was in her past and move on. Somehow she knew what he had found would change all of them. What was there, Lord? I'm talking to You, Paige muttered, but I'm not sure how much I trust.

"Zeke?" She once more looked up at him, tilting her head back. Goodness, she thought, he's tall, well over six foot. What is it with all these tall guys in my life? Her own father was over six foot as well.

He grinned, his hazel eyes sparkling with mischief. "Paige?"

She shook her head. "Okay, so what's the weather to be like tomorrow?"

"It should be okay. I haven't seen signs of any storms moving in. How long will you need?"

"An area this large? Likely three to four days." She chewed at her lip, lost in thought. "I'll need to be in the air as well, and John, the pilot I usually hire, is away until next week."

"We can do the ground work, though, can't we?" Zeke had never been part of what Paige did for a living, but this time, he really wanted to be there. There was something there, he knew, something that would change all their lives.

She thought for a moment, then nodded. "We can start that work. It will take time though. I usually survey from the air first." She turned to stare at Meg. "Meg?"

Meg stared back at her older sister, then nodded. "Please, Paige. I really want to go. You've convinced me that there is a purpose to your work."

Paige finally nodded. "Then, we'll set out first light tomorrow. The days will be long." She traced the route with her finger. "It'll take about thirty minutes to get to where we park the car and then about an hour to get to the edge of where Zeke's looking at. It's not a huge area, but it will take time to assess it." She stood, lost in thought.

Meg and Zeke exchanged a puzzled glance, Meg with more resignation in hers than puzzlement.

"Paige? Come back from wherever you are. We need to plan our trip and you look like you just took off without us?"

❂ ❂ ❂ ❂

The sun had barely peeked over the horizon as Paige shut her vehicle door and stared around. There's something off here, she thought, turning as Zeke walked around the vehicle and stopped in front of her.

"Paige? What now? Where do we head off to?"

She pointed. "That's the trail there." She looked around once more. "I'm glad Meg decided not to come today, to stay in the office." She shivered suddenly and not from cold.

Zeke nodded. "Me, too. I can feel something here." He turned to the back of her vehicle and popped open the hatch, pulling out the two backpacks in it. He shrugged into the heavier one, despite Paige's protests.

"Lead on, Paige. We've what, you said, about an hour's walk?"

She nodded as she adjusted the straps on the backpack, her curls falling across her face and hiding it from Zeke's scrutiny. "About that. I'm still not sure we're doing the right thing though."

Zeke watched what he could of her face, wondering what was really going on. "There's more to this than what happened the other day, isn't there, Paige?"

She stilled in her movements, then sighed, finally nodding. "There is, Zeke.

Just leave it, okay?" She turned and headed away from him, leaving him staring after her.

Running to catch up, he caught her arm, stopping her. "Listen, I didn't mean to pry, but if you ever want to talk, I'll listen."

"Give it a rest, will you?" The anger in her voice bit at him and he took a step back, hands in the air.

"Whatever, Paige. Whatever."

She stalked away from him, angry at herself for reaction. It wasn't his fault, she knew, that she felt the way she did. It was, just what, she couldn't say anymore. She sighed, knowing she would need to apologize but not quite ready to.

An hour later, she paused, her eyes searching the clearing ahead of her, then turning to the sky. Clouds were moving in.

"I thought you said there wasn't rain in the forecast?" She turned to Zeke.

He squinted as he looked up. "Those aren't rain clouds. We'll be fine. No weather expected until tomorrow at the earliest. Okay, so now what?"

"Now what is that I walk the area and search for changes, photographing as I walk. Then I take photos of each area. It's a long process, but not that long if the area we need to look at is small." She paced forward, eyes on the ground. "See this? This has been disturbed recently, and I would say not by animals."

"Human?" At her nod, Zeke spun, looking around him. "I don't like this, Paige."

She shrugged. "I don't either, but we need to do this to find some answers."

Late that afternoon, Zeke handed Paige a bottle of lukewarm water, then took a drink from his own. "It's time we head back down. It's getting dark."

She nodded, her thoughts on what they had found. "I don't like this, Zeke. I'll need to talk to Andrew and have him send someone up to search through this."

"I know." A sound had him turning, then grabbing for their backpacks and Paige's hand, pulling her into the shadows of the trees. "Ssh! I don't like that sound."

They stood and watched as two men approached, then passed by them without speaking. They watched as a hole was dug and something dropped into it. Paige had her camera out, clicking as she watched, her camera on silent mode.

One of the men turned and looked around him. They couldn't hear the conversation but knew they had been tracked that far.

Paige tightened her grip on Zeke's hand, watching as the men studied the ground and then widened their search. Her heart racing, she just stood, until Zeke pulled her with him back more into the forest, leading her towards the trail that would take them back to the vehicle. He pulled her into a run, hoping to put space between them and the men.

Finally, Paige pulled her hand from Zeke's and stopped, bending over to rest her hands on her knees, gasping for air.

"Did we get away, Zeke?"

Zeke searched the area behind him and then looked forward. "For now. I want to know if there's someone waiting down there where the vehicles are. If there is, they'll be looking for us. And if they have contacts, they'll trace your car."

She nodded as she stood. "That's what I'm afraid of. Why did I ever think I could leave the past behind and come home?"

Zeke stared at her. "What do you mean? Leave the past behind? And why not come home?"

She drew a deep breath, opened her mouth to reply and then spun as she heard a sound behind her. She grabbed his hand and started running again, sliding to a halt just before they reached the parking lot, pulling him off into the trees.

Zeke dropped the backpacks and shove Paige behind him, his eyes watchful, ears listening.

"I tell you, there was someone up there when we were. Didn't you hear them running off?"

"You're just imagining things again. There weren't no one there." The second man spit into the forest, his eyes searching around. "If there was, where are they?"

The first man stopped, eyes probing the forest. Zeke felt like he was staring right at them.

"They're here somewhere. That vehicle is still there." He moved towards it, pulling out a weapon. "I want to know whose it is."

Paige gasped, her hand flying to her mouth to silence it, as the men stopped and looked around. Zeke squeezed her hand, eyes watchful.

Finally the men left, and the two in the forest cautiously made their way out to Paige's car.

"Are we safe?" Paige still hesitated even as they loaded the backpacks into the hatch.

Zeke shrugged. "I'm not sure, Paige. We need to go over the photos you took. We're not coming up here again until we do. We need to talk to either Andrew or Bill. The men buried something and I don't think it was legal, not the way they were acting."

Paige shuddered. "I know what you mean." She turned to him, handing him her keys. "Can you drive please?"

Zeke studied her face and saw the fear lurking below the surface. Lord, I have no idea what's going on here or what Paige faced in the past. Be with her right now. Calm her fears. Give her Your peace.

Chapter 4

"Paige. Talk to me. Tell me what happened yesterday out there. You've been locked in here all morning, just staring at those photos." Meg perched on her sister's desk, her slate gray eyes studying her sister.

Paige sighed and sat back, her eyes tracing the photos she had taken, a frown on her face. "We saw someone burying something yesterday and we had to run. I'm not sure if they found out who I am or not. I want you to be very careful, Meg. Watch your surroundings. Stay with Gerry as much as you can when you're out and about."

Meg's eyes grew wide. "What did you see, Paige?"

Paige shrugged. "We're not sure. I'm sending some photos on to Andrew for him to take a look at." She stood and began pacing. "I don't like that danger has come so close to you, Meg."

Meg stood in her sister's path, stopping her. "What danger? You've never ever talked to anyone about why you moved so much. You're looking over your shoulder all the time, Paige. Why?"

Paige shook her head. "I can't tell you. It's safer if you don't know." She looked towards the front of the office. "Someone's just come in, Meg. Go, do what you're supposed to do."

Meg glared at her sister. "This is far from over, Paige. We're not done with this conversation." She walked towards the front. "Jason? Why are you here?"

"I need to talk with Paige. Is she in?"

"Jason? Come on back?" Paige stood in her office doorway. "What's up?"

Jason shot a look back at Meg, who was staring after him and then at Paige. "We need to talk, Paige, in private."

Paige nodded, motioning for him to enter, and then closing the door behind her. "Why?"

"What are you looking into, Paige? What are you mixed up in?" Jason was angry and Paige didn't know if she had seen him like that before.

"Why?"

"Why what? Paige, you need to talk to me. If not me, then Bill or Andrew. That man who was here yesterday? He's been linked to environmentalists who destroy not rebuild our environment. So again, what are you mixed up in?"

Paige shook her head. "Nothing that would have any bearing on this. I just got a call from Zeke, asking me to let him look at some maps and compare them to what he had. I had never met him before."

Jason sighed, running his hand through his hair. "If that's the case, then I need to speak with Zeke and see what he's stirred up." He reached for the doorknob, stopping as Paige spoke.

"We went out yesterday to look at the area he was concerned about. Someone's been burying stuff there. They actually came up there just as we were getting ready to leave."

Jason spun, his eyes hard. "Did you get pictures?"

She nodded. "I was getting them ready to send off to Andrew when you came in. Sit. Look through them. I can forward any to you that you want."

Jason clicked through the pictures, finally stopping at one. "I know these men. They're the ones we're looking for. In fact, one of them was here in your building, looking for your maps." He turned to her, seeing her face whiten. "Now, tell me again, what are you involved in?"

"Nothing, Jason. Absolutely nothing that would have anything to do with this." Her gaze grew distant and he saw the distress in her face before it closed off. "Talk to Zeke. He's the one who stirred all this up."

Jason stood, staring down at her. "I intend you. I don't need to tell you to be very careful, now do I?"

She shook her head. "It's Meg I'm worried about.

❂ ❂ ❂ ❂

Hearing his name called, Zeke looked up to see Jason walking his way. He sighed. Okay, now what? He had had no end of interruptions that day.

"Zeke." Jason stopped beside Zeke and dropped into one of the deck chairs.

"Jason. What brings you out here?"

Jason sighed. "I just spoke with Paige." Jason brought Zeke up to date of where the investigation stood. "So you tell me, what have you gotten mixed up in?"

Zeke shrugged. "I have no idea. All I wanted to do was find out why the area was different from the old maps. What did I walk into?"

Jason shook his head. "We're looking into it. I'm heading up a team that's going out where you two were."

"And just what do you expect to find?"

Jason shrugged. "I have no idea. How about you tell me?"

Zeke stared at him. "Jason, I have no idea." He pointed at his laptop. "I'm trying to work here on something that I have to submit in less than an hour and I have an hour's work on it. How be we leave this conversation for later?"

Jason stood, staring down at his friend. "Stay safe, Zeke. Call me if you need to."

Zeke sat for a moment lost in thought, then shaking his head, immersed himself into his work. Finally he sat back, satisfied with his report and sent it on to the weather station. Being able to freelance was a dream come true for him. He could work from home and that he enjoyed. His thoughts turned to Paige and he spun in his chair to stare the way Jason had walked around his house.

He rose, stretched and entered his back door, heading through to the front. Checking the time, he grimaced. It was past time for Paige to have closed up her office, and he didn't have her address. He did, however, have her cell number.

"Paige? Hi. It's Zeke." He grinned at her surprised voice. "Why am I calling you? I just wanted to know if you had talked to Jason? He did. Okay. So what's the plan then about going back? Supper? Tonight? Sure. Let me have your address."

Zeke pulled into the driveway at Paige's and waited until she had left her vehicle, walking beside her to the door. His hand came out and he stopped her.

"Did you lock your door this morning?"

"I did. Why?" Paige stared at him, then at her front door. "It's open."

"It is. Step back. I'm calling it in."

Paige leaned back against her car, a frown on her face as she watched the officers and the crime scene team once more search a building she knew so well. Who had entered her home?

Zeke stood beside her, arm leaning on the car roof, angled in such a way that he could watch Paige as well as the activity around her. He searched the onlookers, then sighed. He would have no idea of who or what he was looking for.

Andrew, temporary police chief for the town, walked towards her.

"Paige? It's been a while. How are you?"

She snorted. "How do you think I am? My office is tossed, and now my home has been invaded."

Andrew smothered a grin. "Still feisty, are you? You haven't changed."

"We all change, Andrew. What did you find?"

"You're not going to like it. Your place has been tossed and tossed well. What would they have been looking for?"

"The photos I sent you?"

"Photos? From the forest? Those ones?"

She nodded. "Did you get a chance to look at them? Jason did and recognized the two men."

Andrew nodded. "I haven't had a chance to go over them, but I will. Do you think you were seen?"

Zeke spoke up. "I doubt it, but if they have an in, they could find out who she was. More than likely, I would say they've been watching her. They know her vehicle, that's a given."

Paige turned to stare at him. "Meg!"

"Meg is fine. I spoke with her." Andrew turned to look at the house. "You'll be able to go through soon. I want to walk through it with you. Bill's heading up the investigation and will be here as well."

"Investigation?" Paige sighed. "How far does it go?"

"Is there something you're not telling me, Paige? Some reason you should? Maybe we need to talk about why you were running all those years. We've been friends for too long to let anything slip between us."

Zeke watched the conflicting emotions cross her face and saw the moment she caved in.

"I guess I do need to talk to someone. I haven't been able to, not even to Mom and Dad, and especially not Meg." She reached for Zeke's hand and clutched it, not even aware of what she had done. "It's not pretty, Andrew."

"Let's walk through your home first. Then we'll find somewhere to talk."

Paige shook her head. "We talk here or nowhere." She pushed away from the car and headed for the door, Zeke on her heels. Andrew watched, turning as Bill approached him.

"What's going on with Paige?" Bill was puzzled.

"I think we're finally gong to find out. Thing is, I'm not sure if this incident is connected to the other one."

Bill's eyebrow rose. "Two different perps? That's just so helpful, Andrew."

Andrew gave a grim smile. "I know. The one at the office involved Zeke. This one is too personal."

Chapter 5

$\mathscr{P}$aige drew in a deep breath as she straightened back up.   Between the three men and herself, her home was as back to normal as it could be.   She headed for the office and the safe she had hidden there.   It was time to come clean, she thought, and put this nightmare behind her.   It had to have been him that trashed her place, looking for those documents.

She held them, staring down at them, the fear rising once more within her. Had he found her once more? Who could she really trust? A sound at the door had her spinning around to face Zeke.

"Paige?" Zeke's voice was calm as he said her name, not showing the emotions roiling through him.

She sighed. "Zeke. Thanks for the help today. I'm not sure if you'll want to be around me when you hear what I have to say."

"Did you kill someone? Run drugs? Be involved in anything illegal?" When she shook her head, he held out his hand, palm up. "Then, there's nothing to be afraid of. I don't desert my friends." At her questioning look, he sighed. "You know Josiah and Faith? Mark and Julia?" At her nod, he continued, "Josiah and Mark are really good buddies on mine. I helped them when they went through what they went through. Come on, Andrew's waiting for us. Is it really that bad?"

She nodded. "For me it is. You'll not likely think that." She hesitated, then took the hand he offered her, his hand squeezing hers tight.

She sat on the couch, Zeke beside her, her hand still in his. She studied the papers in her hand, finally looking up at Andrew, who sat across from her. She reached them to him.

"Read these first, Andrew. Then we'll talk."

Bill watched the emotions flickering across her face and frowned. His eyes turned to Zeke and caught the look on his face. He sighed to himself. Another one, Lord. Why do they wait until they're in trouble to fall in love?

Andrew scanned the paperwork, then handed it to Bill. "Talk to me, Paige. Explain to me what that's all about."

She sighed, her face going down on her hand, elbow propped on the rough covering on the couch arm. She gripped Zeke's hand tighter.

"Where do I start, Andrew? You know me. You know I never hid anything from my parents, not until that."

"And shame and fear made you, didn't it?"

She nodded, her eyes on him. "They did. I can't do this anymore. I can't run and hide. I thought coming back here, he would leave me alone." She waved her hand around her home. "He hasn't. He was searching for those documents."

Bill looked up from them. "They're forged?"

She nodded. "I never saw them until that night. He had them forged. I checked

47

out the court office when I ran. He was never there."

Zeke reached for the paperwork, his eyes going back to Paige. "Tell us about it, Paige. Let us help you."

She nodded, her eyes on the floor. "I need to go back to college, university, whatever you want to call it. I had a small group of friends and we used to do things together - lunch, supper, outings. There was one fellow there. No one like him and we all tried to avoid him. It wasn't any use. We just couldn't shake him." She stopped, tears gathering in her eyes. They could feel the fear radiating from her.

"One day, I can't even remember what I had been doing, but a few of us met. I was heading to my car when I collapsed. When I woke up, I was in a cabin out in the boonies. He was there, holding up a wedding ring, telling me we had gotten married. He showed me that." She pointed at the papers Zeke held. "I knew it wasn't true. There were too many steps to get a marriage certificate that had to be gone through and I had gone through none of them. We argued. He slapped me around, knocking me down.

He told me I was his and no one else would ever have me. I was petrified. Then, something happened. He seemed to freeze and then dropped to the floor. I was panicking and grabbed up every piece of paper I could find. He was alive when I left, starting to get up. I drove his car as far as the edge of town and then ditched it. I have researched all that and it's all fake."

Zeke's hand tightened on hers some more. "Have you seen him since?"

She nodded. "I would go to a new town, get myself sorted out and start working. Then he'd show up. I moved six or seven times, finally coming back here. I hadn't heard or seen from him in four years. Now this." She raised her eyes to Andrew. "Why now?"

Andrew searched her face, then reached for the paperwork again, slowly reading through it. "This is why. How much do you remember about your Mom's parents?"

She shrugged. "Not a lot. They were both gone before I was ten. Why?"

"Did your parents ever talk to you about a trust fund set up for you and Meg? That comes to you when you turn thirty?"

Paige frowned. "I know there was a trust fund, but I had forgotten about it. Why?"

"Because you're almost thirty and it's due to come to you. Have you any idea how much it's worth?"

She shook her head, then reached for her phone. "Mom would know." She thoughtfully set her phone down when she had finished speaking with her mother. "Did you know, Andrew?"

"I have an idea. Your grandparents were friends with mine. I remember them." He searched her face. "What did your mom say?"

She looked at the three men, shock in her face. "A couple of million, Mom said, maybe more?"

Zeke drew a deep breath. "That's why. Some of this paperwork is a power of financial attorney and another piece is a will. He needed you to sign them in front of a witness. He couldn't forge them. If you were married and something happened to you, then the money would go to him. He just had to wait for what five, six years?"

Bill nodded, having picked up on that. "That's true, Zeke. Now we need to keep you safe from him, as well as from those other men." He turned to Andrew. "Now what?"

Andrew sat back, deep in thought. "It will be tough, Bill." His eyes met Zeke's and he nodded. "I would say, Paige, you just got yourself a boyfriend for the time being, at least until we catch this guy."

Paige spun to stare at Zeke, shaking her head. "I can't put you at risk, Zeke."

Zeke started laughing, drawing a frown from her and grins from the two men. "Paige, I have a dangerous occupation. I go into the midst of storms, tornadoes, what have you as a living."

"That's different. That's your choice."

He put a finger on her lips to silence her. "This is my choice. I want to help you catch not only those ones who broke into your office, but more important. I want this guy."

Andrew watched the interplay between the two, finally speaking.

"Now that you two have come to an agreement, let's make some plans. Bill will look for this man, to see where and what he's up to." He held up a hand as Paige protested. "No, Paige. He kidnapped you and assaulted you. We need to find him. We have no idea how many others he's done this too. Secondly, we need to go forward with our search of that area and for the two men you photographed. Jason's heading out there tomorrow with a team. Are you two free?"

Paige shook her head. "I'm not. Not until afternoon."

Zeke nodded. "I'm working overnight but will be free tomorrow until evening. Then I'm working again."

Andrew searched his face and nodded. "All right. Then we'll plan on you two heading out there tomorrow. I'll arrange for a copter to take you two out there. Paige, you need to talk to your parents and Meg. Warn them. He may try to use them to get to you."

She stared at him, then down at her hands. "He will, won't he?" She rose and walked from the room, coming back with a manila envelope in her hands, handing it to Andrews. "Then that is what this means. I had no idea."

Andrew opened it and pulled out photos of Paige's family. "When did you get this?"

"This morning. I thought it was someone playing a trick on me or something."

"No trick, Paige. This is very real." Bill stood behind Andrew as he flipped through the photos. "We may need to move you to a secure location, if this keeps happening. I'll have someone come by and upgrade your security system here and at your building."

Paige nodded as she sat back down beside Zeke, fright on her face. "He's really serious, isn't he?"

Zeke watched at the two officers searched through the photos, an arm around Paige. "How do we protect her when she's on her own?"

Andrew drew a deep breath. "That's going to be a problem. I need to work on that." He studied Paige, reading her face. "Paige, we've known each other for so many years. Trust me when I say I'll do my best to keep you safe."

"I do, Andrew. I do. It's just…." Her voice died away and she sank deeper into Zeke's hug. "I just want this over. I've been living with this for so many years." She pointed at the paperwork Bill now held. "He's cunning, coming at me when I least expect him." She looked up, both fear and determination in her face. "Why was he silent for those years? Can you find that out?"

Andrew and Bill shared a look. "We'll look into it, Paige. Now, lock up after us. Zeke, you're staying for a while?"

Chapter 6

$\mathscr{P}$aige shifted uncomfortably in the seat at church, Zeke on her one side, Meg on her other, with Meg's boyfriend, Gerry, beside her. She usually enjoyed the services, but today she was restless. She just didn't have the peace she needed to go forward with what she was facing.

Zeke watched Paige's face, knowing she wasn't where she should be in the whole situation. He finally reached an arm around her and hugged her to him, drawing startled eyes to his. He watched as she studied him and saw when she relaxed.

"We'll get him, Paige. We'll get him and you can have your life back."

She nodded, her hair brushing his chin. "I know, Zeke. I just want it over. I don't anyone else hurt."

"It's a risk we take." He pointed to the bulletin she held. "Look what the Scripture passage is this morning."

She stared at him for a moment, then down at the folded paper in her hand. "My peace I give you, not as the world gives, give I unto you."

She sighed, drawing Meg's eyes to her and then to Zeke. "I need that peace, Zeke, oh so badly."

"We'll pray you have it."

After the service, Zeke stood, looking around. He couldn't see anyone out of the ordinary, but then this wasn't the church he normally attended. He turned to Paige, held out his hand and walked away, her hand tucked tight in his.

Two of his friends stood and watched. Josiah and Faith and Mark and Julia exchanged curious glances with one another. Had Zeke found someone at last? Josiah shrugged, then headed after Zeke.

"Hey, Zeke! Wait up!"

Zeke turned at he heard his name called, searching the crowd, his face relaxing when he saw who it was.

"Josiah! What's up?"

"Listen. We're heading back to Mark and Julia's for lunch. Join us."

Zeke looked down at Paige, who had drawn back when Josiah approached. "Paige? My friends would be glad to have us join them or we can do our own thing. It's up to you."

Josiah exchanged a glance with Zeke and nodded. Another lady with a dangerous problem. He sighed. Lord, why is our ladies have to be in danger before we come along? Protect these two.

Paige shrugged. "It doesn't matter, Zeke. Either is fine with me."

Zeke turned his eyes back to hers and studied her for a moment, reading the fear and hesitation in them. "I think we'll join them, Paige. You know both Faith and Julia, I think."

"Faith and Julia? Are you serious?" She stared at Josiah. "Which one?"

"Which one? Oh, I see what you mean. Faith. Julia is Mark's."

She nodded. "Then, we'll be glad to join you four."

Mark and Josiah approached Zeke after the meal, leaving the three ladies talking in the living room. Mark pointed to the back door, closing it behind them.

"What's going on, Zeke? We had no idea you knew Paige?" Mark's voice held a question he didn't ask.

Zeke stared into the distance, as always watching for storm clouds. He really didn't know where to begin or how much he could tell them.

"Zeke?" Josiah spoke up. "What can we do to help you?"

Zeke turned, his eyes on his friends. "I really don't know. This is what is going on and Andrew and Bill are working on it." He laid it all out for them, including the information he had been handed the other night.

"Wow! We had no idea." Mark turned to face the door. "And I'm sure Julia and Faith had no idea. Julia's mentioned that Paige has withdrawn from her friends and she didn't know why. This explains it."

Zeke nodded. "She's trying to keep her friends safe, without realizing what she's doing. Likely, with Julia and Faith being married, they're safe. I hope they can renew their friendship with Paige. She needs that support. She has no idea what your two ladies went through. It might help if she does."

Josiah. nodded. "It might. Let us talk to our ladies and see what we can do about that. Now, about you? Are you okay with this?"

Zeke shrugged. "I have to be. I walked in on the assault. I was with her in the forest that day. I can't just walk away from her."

Josiah and Mark exchanged another glance, smiles lurking on their faces. He sounds just like we both did, doesn't he, Lord, Josiah thought. "Let us know what we can do for you. You've helped both of us out. Prayer is the top priority for now."

Zeke nodded, then headed for the door. "Paige wants to spend some time with her family today. We should likely get moving."

"Zeke?" Paige turned to him as he stopped at a red light. "Did Faith and Julia really go through what they did?"

Zeke nodded. "They did. Faith had a physician stalking her at one point as well. Talk to her. She'll listen, I know."

"How did they manage to stay safe?"

Zeke paused, trying to gather his thoughts. "They didn't, not really. Both were kidnapped, hurt. Julia was going to be sent out of the country, never to come back." He heard Paige's intake of breath. "Both Josiah and Mark stuck it out with them. Our friends helped as well."

"Your friends?"

Zeke grinned. "Yep. You haven't met them all yet, other than Noah, and him you know from growing up here in town."

"Noah's a friend of yours?"

He nodded. "He is. I've asked him to help look into those forged documents. Sometimes he comes across data he doesn't have a clue what to do with and just passes it on to the authorities. I'm praying this is one of those times."

Paige sat back as he stopped in front of her parents. "What do I tell Mom and Dad and Meg?"

"The truth, Paige. Just the truth. They'll understand. They're hurting for you."

"And what do I tell them about you?"

Zeke grinned. "That I really like you and asked you out?"

She smacked his arm. "That's not what happened."

"It isn't?" He grinned at her look. "Listen. They don't need to know you have to have an escort everywhere, although I think your Dad will figure that one out very quickly. Just say I asked you to come out with me and you agreed. Today was the first step in a journey, Paige, that only God knows how long will take. I'm praying it's not a long one."

"Okay." She chewed her lip again, her eyes on the house.

Zeke laid his hand on hers, startling her. "It's okay, Paige. No hand holding. No kisses. None of that unless you agree. You're in charge, do you understand?" At her nod, he continued, "For now, just take my arm. Stay close to me. If I have to grab you and make a run for it, I will. But you decide when we hold hands. Got that?"

She nodded, a sigh coming from her. "Thank you, Zeke. I'm not sure what to expect anymore, after him."

"You haven't dated for years, have you? Didn't think so. We'll just take it one moment at a time, that's all. Sit. Let me open the door for you."

Paige felt Zeke's hand at her back as they walked up the pathway to the door and she stopped, turning to look around her.

"Paige?"

"I can feel him, Zeke. He's out there, watching us. Oh, what did I do? He'll hurt you, and I don't want that." Tears gathered in her eyes at her fright.

Zeke stopped her with a finger to her mouth. "Pray, sweetheart. Pray. God will protect us. He's in control, not this guy."

She nodded, then turned as the door opened and her mother stood there.

"Paige? Are you not coming in at all? And who do you have with you?"

"This is Zeke, Mom. I've told you how he helped clear up the mess in the office the other day." She sighed. "Is Dad home? I need to talk with you two, and I can tell you it's not pretty."

Paige's mother looked at her daughter with a frown, then at Zeke. "He is, honey. Come on in. We're out in the backyard, enjoying the sun. I just hope it doesn't start to rain."

Paige started to laugh as Zeke grinned. Her mother turned to stare at her.

"What did I say, Paige?"

Paige reached to hug her mother. "Just what you said. Zeke's a meteorologist."

Paige's mother stopped, then started to laugh. "Well, I guess I put my foot into that one, didn't I?"

✪ ✪ ✪ ✪

Zeke turned as he heard his name called and saw Bill walking towards him. He sighed. He was on a tight deadline that Wednesday morning, needing to get to the office where he had to do some data input. This would only delay him.

"Bill?"

"Zeke. Just wanted to catch you. I know this is the day you have to be in the office. Walk with me for a moment or two."

"Where do we stand?"

Bill looked up at the sky, then back at Zeke. "He's disappeared, Zeke. We can't find him. And the men in the forest? We've had word they've moved on."

"But you don't think so."

Bill shook his head. "They've gone underground. I wish I knew where. You two need to be very careful."

Zeke nodded. "I know. It's just so hard, Bill."

"It is. How's Paige?"

Zeke shrugged. "How would you expect her to be? Listen. I have to run. Keep me updated, will you?"

Bill watched as Zeke walked rapidly away, his thoughts on the investigation. It's going nowhere, he thought. We have nothing really and that means it will go cold.

I don't like that. He turned to head for the
department.

Chapter 7

$\mathcal{P}$aige stepped back from the table, rubbing her forehead. There was something wrong with her maps, something big, and she just couldn't figure it out. Why not? She blew out a breath, causing her bangs to flutter.

"Meg? Do you have a moment?"

Meg peeked into the room. "What's up, Paige?"

"Take a look at these maps, will you? Tell me what different about them."

"You want me to tell you what's wrong with your maps?" Meg's eyes popped wide.

Paige nodded. "I do. There's something there, and I can't see it."

Meg studied the map and then the photos, finally pointed along an area. "There. That's what's difference. In your photos, it looks as if it's been dug up and recently at that. Paige, what's going on?"

Paige studied the area Meg was pointing at and sighed. "You're right, Meg. That's what was puzzling me. I need to talk with Andrew."

"Paige?" Meg moved in front of her sister to stop her. "What's going on?"

Paige studied her face, then sighed. "Something I don't want you mixed up in. It's too dangerous."

"But it's not too dangerous for you?"

Paige shook her head. "I'm not saying that, Meg. What I am saying is that I may become a target and I don't want you to become one as well."

Meg watched as Paige rolled up her maps and grabbed her photos, heading for the outside door. "Paige? Where are you going?"

"To find Andrew. I need to show him these." Paige stopped as she looked out the window to the parking lot, then reached to lock the door. She almost ran back to her office. "Meg, grab your stuff. We need to leave and leave now."

"Paige?"

"Just do it. We're going out the back and heading away from here." Paige grabbed a garbage bag and stuffed the paperwork into it. "Here, you take this and run. I'll head the other way. They're after me, not you. Find Andrew."

Paige bolted through the back door, shoving Meg ahead of her, pointing towards the downtown area. Meg gave an anguished look at her sister and then grasping the bag in one arm, took off. Paige heard shouts from the front of the building and hesitating until she was seen, took off in the opposite direction from Meg. She could hear pounding footsteps behind her as she desperately searched for a hiding spot. Seeing none, she kept running, the footsteps getting closer.

She felt herself shoved down, face ground into the earth, and a heavy knee on her back. She struggled to get away as her arms were grasped and pulled behind it.

"Where is it?" the deep growl sounded in her ear.

"I don't know what you want." Still struggling, she felt her face shoved even further into the ground.

"The maps and photos. Where are they?"

She shook her head. "I don't know what you want. Let me go!"

She was hauled to her feet, a blindfold slapped across her eyes and then propelled to a vehicle she could hear running near her. She was shoved into the back seat, her arms tied behind her. She listened but didn't hear any words spoken between her captor and the driver. Just how many men were there? Lord, I'm in over my head. I need Your help.

Zeke slid to a halt, too late to intervene. His heart dropping, he tried his best to memorize the plate number as he pulled out his phone and called in the abduction.

Bill walked towards him ten minutes later. Zeke stood, hands jammed into his pockets, eyes searching the direction the car had disappeared to.

"Zeke?"

Zeke didn't turn, didn't take his eyes off the distance. "Bill? What do you have?"

"The plate number is to a stolen car."

"Of course it is. Why wouldn't it be?" He turned his head to study his friend. "Where is she?"

Bill sighed. "We have no idea."

Zeke nodded. "What did they want?"

"Meg ended up at the department looking for Andrew. Paige stuffed maps and photos into a garbage bag and sent her to him before she took off the other way."

Zeke stilled, then pulling out his right hand, running it through his hair. "The forest. They wanted the maps and the photos we took. How did they know she had them?" He turned to face Bill. "It's my fault. I asked her to look into this."

Bill watched as emotions flickered across Zeke's face. "She could have said no to your request, Zeke. What we need to concentrate on now is finding her."

"She said she emailed the photos to Andrew. Has he looked at them?"

Bill shook his head. "He's been away over the last couple of days. He had something he had to take care of. He's back in the office now." He pulled out his phone. "Andrew? Bill. Yeah, I'm on the scene, but there's not a lot of evidence, I doubt. Did you get that email from Paige? You did. And? All right. Zeke's with me. We'll head your way."

Zeke studied his friend. "What did Andrew say?"

"He wants to talk to you, Zeke. Something about the photos. He has the documents Meg delivered. He's sent someone with her to the office, to search it as well."

"How's Meg?"

"She's scared, Zeke. Terrified is the word Andrew used. He's sending an officer to her parents' place as well." He searched the area. "Someone's out there, Zeke, out there watching us."

"I know. I'd like to get my hands on him." Zeke was angry and knew he needed to calm himself down.

"Let God deal with your anger, Zeke. Remember what the pastor said yesterday, ask God for peace in every situation."

Zeke sighed. "I know. It's okay to say in principle, but so hard to put into practice."

Andrew looked up as Bill and Zeke appeared in the doorway to the board room he was in. He motioned them in and then shut the door.

"How's Meg?" Zeke was concerned about her.

"She's scared, Zeke. I have a female officer with her right now. They've gone back to the building, to help the search there. Your girlfriend's good, you know. She handed this off to her sister and sent her to me." Andrew held up a hand as Zeke protested. "I know. She should have just called for help, but I doubt she would have had time. She locked the door and from what I gather has been found, it was kicked in and they followed them through the building."

Zeke nodded. "But where are we in trying to find her? Bill said the car was stolen."

Andrew shot a look at Bill, who shook his head. "It was, Zeke. It's standard in cases like this. Steal a car to commit a crime." He turned back to the maps and photos. "Meg said she found what was puzzling Paige. This spot right here. Is that where you saw them digging?"

Zeke moved closer to the maps and studied them. "No. It was more to the left." He pointed to the area. "Right there. What were they burying?"

"Containers of contaminants. Deadly products from what the lab has said. We're trying to track the exact composition of it and where they likely came from."

"Contaminants?" Zeke's voice was puzzled. "Wow!" He pulled out his phone as it chimed. "Sorry, guys. I need to run. I have to be in the office in thirty."

"Bill here goes with you. Someone will be with you at all times, Zeke." Andrew stared him down, waiting until Zeke nodded. "It's for your safety. If they suspect that you're involved and I'm sure that they do, they'll come after you as well."

Chapter 8

A week later, Meg looked up from her desk in the office as Zeke walked in. Her face was haggard as was his.

"Any news, Zeke?"

He shook his head as he perched on the corner of her desk. "Come on, Meg. Let me take you home. I talked to your Mom and Dad. They're closing the office for now, until Paige comes back."

"And is she coming back, Zeke?"

He nodded. "She will, Meg. Keep that faith."

She rose and followed him out of the building, locking it behind her. She stopped, looking around, a shiver running through her.

"Meg?" Zeke watched her face.

"Someone's out there, Zeke. Who is it?"

Zeke nodded. "I know. Come on, Meg. Let's get you home."

Zeke walked back through the forest. He had come out to the area Paige had photographed, just to see what he could find. Hearing a noise he looked up to see two men in hoodies approaching him. He stopped, hands going up in the air.

The shorter man spoke. "We're not your enemies, Zeke. We want to help but we need your help and Paige's help."

"Like Paige can help right now?" Zeke frowned, trying to catch any glimpse of the men's faces.

"She will. Trust me on that. We need your help to stop the men ruining the land around here. They're planting contaminants to destroy the land so they can buy it up cheap."

"Go to the authorities."

"We can't, not just yet. We don't have enough evidence and the ones involved are prominent in town."

"So?"

"We need you to find us the evidence." He nodded past Zeke at the newly turned earth. "That's part of it. You and Paige stumbled onto it. We need you to continue to follow it up."

Zeke shook his head. "Not happening. Not until Paige comes back. So release her."

The man looked past Zeke towards the edge of the forest. "We don't have her and we don't know where she is. That's what you and the police need to figure out. What you need to do as well is follow the clues to who is the head of this group."

The men turned and walked away, leaving Zeke staring after them. A sound behind him had him spinning that way. No one was there but he knew someone had been.

The man who had stood at the edge of the forest lowered his hoodie and stared back at Zeke from the depths of the forest. He prayed that Zeke would help. He was the only one he knew that could help his group stop this.

Zeke headed back for his vehicle, lost in thought. Where is she, Lord? It's been a week and we're not closer to finding her. Protect her. Help her to find peace in whatever she's involved in. Bring her home safely.

✿ ✿ ✿ ✿

Paige stood at the window of the second floor bedroom she was confined to. She could see one of her captors making his rounds in the yard. She leaned her head against the glass and sighed. It had been how long now, she thought. When do I get to go home, Lord? They keep asking me for information that I can't give them.

A sound at the door had her turning that way. A tray slid through the open door and she heard the lock click in place. This repeated itself three times a day. She refused to eat, refused to drink what they provided. She couldn't be sure it wasn't drugged.

A sound in the next room caught her attention and she spun to look at the wall, a frown in place. What was going on, she wondered? Then she shrugged, her eyes going back to the outside. Somehow she had to get away, and she wasn't sure how she would. Lord, guide me in this please? I want to get away, but I just don't know how I can.

Paige ignored the sound of the door unlocking, just as it had for the past week or more. She had lost track of the days. Tired from not sleeping and not eating, she had no fight left in her.

Footsteps neared her and then stopped, waiting for her to turn. When she didn't, her arm was grasped and she was roughly pulled around, to face a man with a mask on. She saw the glittering angry blue eyes staring at her.

"Where are the photos and the maps?"

She shook her head. "I don't know. I don't have them."

She tasted the blood on her lip from the blow across her face. Smart one, girl. She shook her head. "As far as I know the police have them." She stared at the hatred and anger in the eyes facing her. As the door lock clicked closed, she picked herself up, hand to her face. Another bruise, she thought. Just what I needed. She rested her head against the window, eyes staring into the distance. When, Lord? When do I get out of here?

Zeke walked towards his home, eyes searching the sky. A storm was moving in and he needed to be alert and ready to watch it. He needed to send in the information they needed at the meteorology office to confirm the predictions and weather systems, but his heart wasn't in it. When, Lord? When will Paige come home? She has my heart, Lord, took it when I wasn't looking. Bring her back to me.

He turned as he heard sirens and saw a cruiser speeding from town followed by a paramedic unit. His heart lifted in prayer for those involved. His phone chimed and he ignored it. He needed to work and interruptions wouldn't get his forecast and observations done.

Late that night, a knock came to his door. He sighed, looking at the clock. It was late and he was just finished his work. He needed some down time but chances were he wasn't going to get it. He listened to the sound of the heavy rain and wind and wanted to be out in it somewhere, somewhere he could lose himself for a while.

He stared at Jason standing at his door, then moved aside so his friend could enter. Jason shook his hat out the door, and then looked ruefully down at the rain dripping onto the floor.

"Sorry about this, Zeke."

"Not a problem, but what are you doing out here so late?" Zeke studied the eyes raised to his, a whisper of hope coming to his heart.

"We have Paige, Zeke. Josiah and Faith were driving out of town this afternoon, heading for who knows where so she could take some photos to work into stained glass. Faith saw what she thought was a blanket at the side of the road and made Josiah stop. It was Paige."

Zeke stared at him. "Is she alive?" At Jason's nod, his eyes slid closed. "Thank you, Lord." Then his eyes popped open. "How bad?"

"Not as bad as we thought. Some bruising. The doctor doesn't think she's eaten at all or drank much the whole time she's been gone. She was also drugged before she was dumped. Come on. I'll take you to her. Her parents asked me to come get you."

Zeke reached for his jacket and cap, then turned to the kitchen, locking the door he had left open. Pulling the front door closed and checking that it was locked, he started down the walk, then stopped. He could feel someone there, someone who had been haunting his every step.

"Zeke?" Jason returned to stand in front of Zeke. "What's wrong?"

Zeke shrugged. "I just feel someone out there, someone watching me all the time."

Jason nodded. "There likely is. Come on. Let's get you to your lady."

Zeke walked down the hospital corridor, dimmed now for the night, his booted heels clicking with each step. He stopped at the door with the police guard. He hesitated until the officer smiled and pushed the door open for him. Paige's parents looked up and Meg rushed to him, enveloping him in a hug, tears on her face.

"She's back, Zeke. Just like you said."

Arm around Meg, Zeke walked to the foot of the bed, his eyes on Paige. Wincing at the bruising on her face, he watched, eyes devouring the woman he knew he loved.

Paige's mother, Anna, spoke. "Zeke, she was awake and asking for you."

Zeke's eyes turned to Anna. "She was? Did she say why?"

Anna shook her head. "No. She was out again before we could do more than tell her we would send for you." Anna shared a look with her husband, David, and then stood. "You stay for a while, Zeke. We're going to go see if we can find something to eat." She stopped to give him a hug. "Thank you, Zeke."

She was gone before Zeke could say a word, leaving him staring after her. He finally moved to sit where Anna had been sitting, his hand reaching for Paige's, enveloping it in his warm grasp. He felt her fingers tighten, and he looked up. Her eyes were open but not focused.

"I need to find Zeke. He's not safe. They're looking for him. I need to get out of here." She shoved at the blankets, trying to rise.

Zeke rose, his hand going to her arm, whispering quietly to her. She finally relaxed, eyes closing. Zeke sat back down, eyes on her face, wondering what had happened to her over the last eight days. Something had, and he wanted those responsible to pay.

Chapter 9

Paige's eyes fluttered open and she stared around, fear coursing through her. She didn't know where she was. Feeling a pull on her arm, she raised her hand. An IV? Where? Turning her head, she squinted through the dimmed light to see who was sitting beside her. Zeke? Where had he come from?

Zeke raised his head as he heard Paige stirring, his eyes blinking as he came awake. He rose and leaned on the side bedrail, watching as she fully roused.

"Paige? How are you feeling?"

She shook her head, her mouth and throat dry, unable to speak.

"Here. They said you could have sips of water when you roused." He held the glass to her mouth, letting her sip through the straw. "Welcome home."

"Where?"

"You're in our hospital, Paige. Josiah and Faith found you. Ssh! The doctors don't want you talking a lot yet. You need to rest and get some strength back." He watched as fear coursed through her eyes, and they lit on the door. "We have a guard out there. Andrew's posted one at the door and one in the waiting room. No one gets in to you that's not on his approved list."

"Mom and Dad? Meg?"

"They're fine. They'll be back in a couple of hours. Your Dad took them home to get some sleep." He reached for her hand, his thumb rubbing a circle on the back of it. "I'm glad you're home. You had me so worried."

She gave a half smile. "Did they catch the men?"

"Not yet. You weren't with them when you were found."

Frowning, she stared at the door, willing answers to come. "I don't remember that. Last I remember I was in the bedroom they put me in, staring out the window, trying to figure out how to escape."

"Andrew and Bill are wanting to talk with you."

She nodded, then yawned, her eyes sliding close as she slept. Zeke watched her for a few minutes, then sought his chair, eyes not leaving her face. *Lord, where was she? How do I help her now? She didn't have peace before, so how does she find Your peace now?*

Andrew peeked around the door a couple of hours later, then walked into the room on soft-soled shoes.

"Morning, Zeke. Has she been awake?"

Zeke stretched as he nodded. "For a few minutes. She didn't remember much, though."

Andrew shook his head. "And she told you that?"

Zeke gave a grim smile. "She did. She says she remembers being in a bedroom trying to find a way out and then nothing."

"That's highly likely, given she was drugged." Andrew waited for a while, then turned. "Call me when she wakes up."

Zeke nodded and watched as Andrew walked away. Now what, he wondered? Where do we go from here?

He finally rose, heading for the door, stopping to take a look back at Paige. He sighed, torn. He wanted to stay with her, but he also needed to be out there doing his job. There was a huge weather system moving in and he wanted to be part of it. He finally left, heading for the elevator and then the outside, stopping as he remembered he didn't have his car. Jason had brought him to the hospital last night. He sighed, pulling out his phone and scrolling through to find a number of someone he could call.

"Zeke?"

His head shot up at the call. Adam, a good friend, stood there.

"What are you doing here? Aren't you constructing or building or reno'ing something?"

Adam laughed. "I'm waiting on some supplies to come in. Jason called, said you needed a ride and he didn't figure you would remember until you hit the parking lot that you didn't have your vehicle."

Zeke laughed. "He was right. Where are you parked?"

"Illegally I think. Right over here." When they were seated in the vehicle, Adam asked, "How's Paige?"

Zeke shrugged, not quite sure how to respond. Her words from the night before still echoed through his mind. "She was sleeping when I left. She was awake in the night, for a bit." He turned to Adam. "Tell me, again, exactly why you're here."

Adam shook his head as he grinned. "I told you. Jason asked if some of us could stay with you until they get this sorted out with Paige."

Zeke stared at him. "That's not happening, Adam. You all have your own work to do. I'm sure you have something you could be working on, even while waiting for supplies to arrive."

"Let's just say I'm happy to help out a friend. Now, where are we heading? You look as if you could use a shower and a change of clothes."

"Smart mouth!" Zeke shook his head. "Take me home, James."

Adam started laughing even as he protested that he was not a chauffeur.

Later that morning, Adam approached Zeke as he stood, eyes on the sky and a frown on his face. "You don't look happy, Zeke."

Zeke turned. "I'm not. The system that's moving in has already spawned heavy rain and winds and even tornadoes. It's heading right our way, and I'm afraid people aren't taking the warning seriously. They never do here, thinking it will hit somewhere else." He paused. "I'm afraid that it will wash away the evidence we found and that the police left in place."

"Not much we can do about that, is there? They left it there for a reason. I'm sure they have taken all the pictures and evidence they needed before they left."

Zeke sighed. "They did. Now, let's head out of town."

✪ ✪ ✪ ✪

Paige stirred finally, her eyes gradually opening and focusing. She searched the room, finding the face of her mother.

"Mom?"

"Paige! You're awake. Thank you, Lord." Anna reached to touch her daughter's face, careful to avoid the bruise. "How are you feeling?"

"Sore and thirsty." She drank as her mother held the glass to her mouth. "Where's Dad and Meg?"

"They're in the cafeteria. They'll be back shortly. Andrew's been around. He'll be back to question you shortly, he said."

Paige stared at her mother, then shook her head. "It's not use, Mom. I don't know anything. I can't remember anything."

"That's fine. Just tell him that. Zeke was here overnight with you, you know."

Paige's eyes shot to her mother. "Oh, no!. He can't come near me. They threatened him."

"Paige?" Her mother wrapped her in a hug as tears flowed down Paige's face. "You remember that?"

Paige nodded. "I do. Please. Don't let him near me."

"We can't keep him away, Paige, no matter what you say. Andrew wants to keep you two together as much as he can. He says it's easier to watch the two of you if you're together."

Zeke stood in the open doorway, one hand on the door, the other holding flowers, listening to what Paige had said. He moved forward, drawing her eyes to him. Her head shaking, she swiped at the tears on her face.

"Anna, can you give us a moment, please?" Zeke appealed to Anna, who nodded and walked away.

Zeke moved to the side of the bed, laying the bouquet on the pillow beside Paige, then reaching for her hand. He refused to release it as she tugged on it.

"Zeke! Please! You need to stay away from me."

"Not happening, Paige. You and I are in this together and for the long haul. I thought I had lost you for good." Zeke watched as she still shook her head, not looking at him. "Paige, look at me. Paige!"

The harshness in his voice drew her eyes to him and she saw the love and compassion reflected there. She still shook her head but not as vigorously.

"Zeke, I don't want you hurt."

"Think about it, Paige. If I hadn't been poking around and asked you to study those maps for me, none of this would have happened.   You wouldn't be hurt and I would never have met you."

She stared at him, then sighed. "You're right, I know. What am I going to do with you?"

He smiled, then handed her the bouquet. "Take these for starters." He watched as she touched the flowers, then looked up at him, a smile in place.

"Thank you, Zeke. Did we just go somewhere else in our friendship?"

Zeke shrugged. "Is there a problem with giving a friend flowers?"

She shook her head. "No, and I thank you. Just checking."

"Keep checking then. We're working through where we're heading. And don't think I plan on walking away. Ever."

Paige's eyes shot to him. "Thank you, Zeke. I just don't want you hurt."

"I can't begin to tell you how I felt the last few days when you were missing. Don't disappear again. My heart can't take it." He looked behind him as the door cracked open. "Andrew. You're back."

Andrew laughed. "That I am. Paige, how are you feeling now?"

She shrugged. "How would you expect me to feel?" She clutched the flowers tight until Zeke loosened her fingers, taking the flowers and searching for a vase in the bedside table, not finding one.

"So, Paige. Talk to me. Tell me what you remember."

Paige stared at Andrew, her brow furrowed. "I don't remember a whole lot, other than many hours standing at a window, staring out, trying to figure out how to get out of a second-story room. They wanted the photos and the maps."

Andrew nodded. "That's what we figured. They're safe. Meg has made a backup of the photos from your computer and then deleted them. That backup is safe, and I'm not telling you where. Can you describe the men in any way?"

She shook her head. "Not really. They just shoved my food through the door three times a day. And asked through the door where the photos and maps were." She stopped, her eyes darkening. "Until the last day. A man came in and asked me. He was shorter than you and stocky. Blue eyes but I couldn't see anything else. That's the last I remember."

"What did you see out the window?"

"Other than men patrolling the yard? Not a lot. We weren't in town, I don't think. There didn't seem to be a lot of houses around." She looked up at Andrew. "Why did they let me go?"

Andrew sighed, knowing he would have to share his supposition with the two. "When you refused to turn over the photos and the maps, we think they let you go so that you would lead them to where you stashed them. You don't have them and that worries me." He didn't add what Bill and he had talked about, that because she refused to cooperate, they just wanted to get rid of her and dumping her on an unused roadside seemed to be their best plan.

Paige shook her head. "I don't want to know where they are. But tell me. How is the investigation going into them?"

Andrew stared at her, then at Zeke. "We're moving ahead, but it's a slow process, as I'm sure you understand." He paused, not quite sure how to proceed. "That other matter? He's dropped out of sight, but I heard from a street cop that he's been seen in town. You need to be extremely careful, Paige. Stick with Zeke as much as you can. Maybe, just maybe, if he thinks you've moved on, he will too."

Paige shook her head. "That's not him. He'll still come after me, even just for revenge because I got away." She sighed, her head going back on her pillow. "Why me?"

Chapter 10

Zeke sat at the crossroads, studying the sky. He finally made a turn and then parked, exiting his vehicle, eyes to the sky. He could see the huge cloud formation moving in. What would it bring, Lord? Rain, thunderstorms, or something much more sinister? He turned to look back towards the town he now called home. Their emergency plan seemed to be non-existent. That wasn't good, he thought. Who could he talk to about that? Jason would know.

He returned to his vehicle and pulled away to come to a stop further down the road where he once more got out and stared at the sky, not seeing the truck that had pulled out behind him. He was being followed and didn't even know it. The truck passed him, then slowed and stopped.

Zeke stopped walking, his eyes going to the truck ahead of him, watching as two men exited.   Now what, Lord, he asked? Who are these men?

"Can I help you?"   Zeke stepped backwards as they approached.

"Are you Zeke Williams?"   The shorter man of the two approached, stopping just feet in front of Zeke.

"And who's asking?"   Zeke kept his eyes on the first man, even as the second man moved to flank him. Okay, Lord, what did I get myself into, he asked?

"We have a message for you."

Zeke felt the blow to his back and was down on his knees, his face crumpled in pain, one hand reaching for the area.   He didn't see the kick that came from the front, catching him in the ribs and knocking him to the ground.   The men finally walked away, leaving Zeke sprawled facedown near the ditch, eyes closed.

❂ ❂ ❂ ❂

Paige looked up from her work as Meg stopped in her doorway, a puzzled look on her face.

"Paige, are you done for the day?"

Paige looked at the clock and then nodded. "I am, by the looks of the clock. Help me straighten up and we'll leave." She stared at her sister. "There's something else, isn't there?"

Meg nodded. "I thought Zeke was coming by today to take you out to lunch."

Paige stood for a moment, lost in thought. "He was." She reached for her phone, scrolling through her messages and missed calls. "Not a word from him." She shrugged. "With the weather gathering, I would suspect he's been too busy. Now, you get out of here. You have plans for tonight?"

Meg smiled. "We do. We're heading to the program at the church."

"Good. I may see you there, if Zeke comes by."

Paige didn't let on to her sister she was very worried. Where was Zeke? It was so unlike him not to call or send a text message at some point during the day. This was the first day he hadn't since they met.

Paige dialled Zeke's number, listening as it went to voice mail. A text message went unanswered. She stared out the window at the pouring rain, finally grabbing an umbrella and running for her car. She had a bad feeling about this.

"Andrew? It's Paige. Have you talked to Zeke today? You haven't, huh? No. I haven't seen him. We were to go out for lunch but he never showed. Do I know where he was heading this morning? No, I don't, I'm sorry. Okay. If I hear from him, I'll call you. It's just not like him, that's all."

❂ ❂ ❂ ❂

The heavy rain and wind made it difficult for Josiah and Jason to see. They were on a hunt and had been since Andrew had called. They needed to find Zeke but had no idea where he was.

Jason finally stopped his truck, straining to see through the rain. Even on high, the wipers weren't much use.

"Which way, Josiah? I feel like we're in the right area. I'm just not sure where to go from here." Jason turned to his friend, seated beside him.

99

"Let's go to the right. This road ends about a mile down there. If we don't see anything, we'll head the other way."

Jason made his turn, creeping along as they both tried to watch the road and the sides along it.

"Wait! Isn't that Zeke's vehicle?" Josiah pointed.

"It is. Let me pull in front of it." Jason stopped, then grabbed up his phone. "Andrew? We've found his truck just now. We're heading out to scour the area. I would say it's been here for a while though. Where? Church Farm Lane - about a mile east of the crossroads. Yeah, we'll likely need paramedics. You're heading this way? Great!"

Josiah stepped from the truck pulling his slicker hood over his cap. Not that it helped any, with the wind blowing the rain into his face. Conversation was difficult and they had to resort to hand signals. Jason approached Zeke's vehicle, trying the doors. He was surprised to find the driver's door open. Checking inside, he shook his head at Josiah.

"He's not there. Where is he?"

"It's too dark for us to split up. We'll have to work together." Josiah took the flashlight he was handed, hunching his shoulders against the rain and wind. "How long do you think he's been parked here?"

Jason turned to look behind the truck. "It was before the rain started and that was early afternoon. There are no tracks in the mud."

Neither said a word, afraid for their friend. Okay, Lord, where is he? Josiah turned to walk along the road, near the ditch. He stumbled suddenly and dropped to his knee, his flashlight rolling from his hand. He stood and reached for the light, his hand stilling as he saw a dark mass lying in front of him. Shining the light towards the ground, he froze.

"Jason! Over here! I've found him."

Josiah dropped to his knees, hand reaching for Zeke. He was alive, but soaking wet and unconscious.

Jason took one look and ran for his truck, pulling out a blanket and then a tarp.

"Here. Cover his with the blanket, Josiah, and then we'll put the tarp over him as much as we can. I know he's soaked, but let's try and keep as much more rain off him as we can."

Josiah nodded, helping to spread the blanket, then shook his head. "It's too windy, Jason. We'll never keep the tarp over him."

They both turned as they saw the flashing emergency lights. Andrew ran towards them.

"Is it Zeke?" At their nod, he stared at them, then dropped to a knee beside Zeke, trying to assess him. "Let me have your light. You just found him?"

"Just long enough to put the blanket on him.'

Andrew shone the light towards Zeke's face. "It's no accident, fellows. There's too much bruising on his face."

He stood and watched as the paramedics worked over Zeke, wiping away the rain that fell on his face with an upraised arm.

"Jason, head for Paige and get her to the hospital. Josiah, bring Zeke's truck."

Andrew stared through the rain. Someone was watching, he could tell, he just couldn't see where that person was. Who is it, Lord? And will Zeke even survive? He's been out in this cold rain for so long.

Andrew followed the stretcher as Zeke was pushed into the Emergency Department, his eyes watchful. He had a call into Zeke's parents but they hadn't called him back yet. He needed to know who was next of kin for power of attorney. The physicians would want to know that, he knew.

He stopped as he saw Josiah approaching. "It's after midnight, Josiah. Why don't you head home?"

Josiah shook his head. "Not until I know how he is. He was beaten, Andrew?"

"From the little I could see of his face, I would say so. The paramedics didn't see any wounds on his hands, so it looks as if he didn't get a chance to defend himself."

Josiah shook his head again. "Who?"

"That's what we'll be trying to find out." Andrew spoke in a grim manner, eyes once more going to the cubicle Zeke lay in.

Paige sat in her living room, staring out the window, her hand absently brushing across her cat's fur. *Where is Zeke, Lord? I know something has happened to him.* She started as she saw lights cross her front window where she had left the curtains open to watch the sky.

A knock at the door had her up and at it, her hand to her throat. Asking who it was, she threw the door open and drew Jason in.

"Jason?" Fright crossed her face as she saw the stern lines on his.

"We've found him, Paige. He's hurt and has been lying out in the elements. Come. I'll take you to him."

"But I'm not a relative." She protested even as she reached for a jacket.

"No, but you're his lady. That's what counts right now. Andrew's trying to reach his family but hasn't heard back from them." Jason stole a quick glance at his watch. It was now early morning. How long had Zeke been unconscious? They might never know. Andrew had let him know the physician was concerned enough that it made Andrew worry.

Jason hurried Paige into the waiting room area and then went to find Andrew. He stopped as he saw the grim lines had deepened on Andrew's face.

"Andrew?"

Andrew turned at Jason's voice, his eyes glimpsing Paige standing in the waiting room. "Jason. It's not good."

"How bad is he?"

"Another thirty minutes and the physician thinks he would have been dead. He's been severely beaten. That alone is bad enough but he's been out in the rain since it started. They're trying to warm him now, in-between X-Rays and what have you."

"Did you get in touch with his family?"

Andrew nodded. "I did. Apparently, Zeke changed his power of attorney recently. To Paige."

Shocked, Jason stared at Andrew and then back at Paige. "I don't think she knows that."

Andrew shook his head. "I don't think she does either. It's just been done in the last couple of days, since Paige was kidnapped."

They walked towards Paige, seeing her hands clench together even tighter. Andrew's hand on her shoulder drew her to a chair and he gently pushed her down.

"Andrew?"

Andrew sat, fatigue setting in. "Paige, he's been beaten and been out in the elements. They're still running tests on him." He stopped, eying her face. "I have a question for you, though. I talked to Zeke's parents. Apparently, he's changed who he has done as his contact for medical emergencies."

"He has?" Paige was surprised. "Who is it?"

"You."

"Me?" Paige's voice ended in a squeak. "That can't be right. I'm not family."

"No, you're not. Not yet." She stared at him, her mouth open. He tapped her chin to close it. "Zeke wouldn't have done that unless you meant everything to him. That's just who he is and how he thinks."

Paige sat back, eyes staring at Andrew and then at Jason. "Why? We're just friends."

Jason gave a tight smile. "That's what you may think, Paige, but if you really did think it through, you would see that Zeke has crossed the line from just friends to much more. He's holding back, waiting on you."

Paige shook her head. "That's not right. He wouldn't do that."

Andrew gave a tired smile. "Whether you think it's right or not, Paige, it's a done deal. The physician will be out shortly to speak with you." Andrew sat back, fatigue drawing from his last reserves. It had been a brutal day and wasn't over yet.

Jason slumped in the chair on the other side of Paige, his eyes drifting closed. He had been up almost twenty-four hours and he would soon need to head out on his shift. He looked up as someone stopped in front of them.

"Mark? What are you doing here?"

"Julia sent me. Maria had called her."

Jason nodded as his brother-in-law sat beside him. His head drooped and he slept. Josiah had headed home, asking them that they kept him updated.

Chapter 11

*H*earing footsteps approached, Paige raised her head from where it had been resting on Andrew's shoulder. Blinking, she looked up at the physician standing, his eyes hooded as he stared at her.

"Paige?"

"Jim Watson? Is that you? I didn't know you were back in town."

"I have been for the last year. Working in the Emergency Department hasn't left a lot of time to look up old friends." He stopped, looking behind him. "I understand that Zeke Williams is a friend of yours?"

She nodded, a frown on her face, not quite knowing what he was asking.

"You have power of attorney for medical purposes for him?"

"I do. Why?"

"We're needing to take him to surgery. I have requested the on-call surgeon to come in. Zeke is bleeding from his spleen and we need to address that."

Paige stood. "I want to see him."

Jim nodded. "I'll take you to him." He stopped as the three men with Paige rose. "You're all together?"

Andrew spoke up. "Jason and I are police officers. Mark's a good friend. I would rather that Paige not be out of the sight of Jason or myself."

Jim studied him, then nodded. "All right. Only one of you though."

Andrew nodded and headed back with Paige.

Jim stopped Paige before she ducked behind the curtain to be with Zeke. "Paige, before you go to him, you should be aware that he has been very badly beaten. We also have the length of time he was out in the elements to deal with. Just be prepared for the cuts and bruises you are going to see." Jim shared a look with Andrew over her head.

She nodded, then reached for the curtain, hesitation in her movements. *What did he go and do that for, Lord? We're nowhere near that close. At least I didn't think we were.* She sighed, knowing she would have to work that through at some point. Right now, she just wanted to go and see him. Andrew's hand on her back gave her the confidence she needed, and she pushed past the curtain.

She stopped, her hands going to her mouth, tears in her eyes as she saw Zeke. The vivid bruising and cuts covered most of his face. She walked forward, her pace slow, stopping as she reached the stretcher. Her hand went out to gently touch his face and then she reached for his hand, her eyes turning to the monitors and then the lines running into Zeke's body.

"What do I need to sign, Jim? You said you were looking at surgery."

Jim nodded, his head turning as an older man entered, reaching to shake his hand. "Paige, this is John Walker. He's the surgeon I said would be in. Now, we need a few moments with Zeke. You can wait right outside the curtain. We'll call you back in soon."

Andrew wrapped an arm around Paige and held her up as she broke down in silent sobs. He heard footsteps and knew Jason and Mark had come close.

"Andrew?" Jason's voice was quiet.

"It's okay, guys. The surgeon's with him." He looked around. "Listen, Mark, you head on home. We'll call once we know something more. Jason, you need to head home to Maria. I've arranged for someone to cover your shift today."

The two men were hesitant to leave but nodding, headed out. Paige watched them walk away, then her eyes went back to the curtain. Please, Lord, don't take him from me. Please!

"Paige? You can come back in. We need to talk to you." Jim had pulled back the curtain and was watching her, an unreadable look on his face.

"Jim?" Andrew's hand on her elbow kept her upright.

"This is Paige Matthews, Zeke's lady."

John Walker stared at her, then back at Zeke. "We have a difficult situation here, Paige. We need to take him to the operating room. His spleen has been lacerated and he's losing blood. That has to be addressed. However, we have the complications of his exposure to the elements. We can't guarantee that he'll even come through the surgery, but he won't live if we don't. The bleeding is extensive."

Paige nodded, having already prayed it through. "Surgery, Dr. Walker. At least that way he has a chance. He's in God's hands."

Dr. Walker looked at her, then at Andrew, and nodded. "As you say, he is. We'll be taking him up shortly. You can with him until then. After that, you can wait in the surgical waiting room." He turned to Andrew. "I hear his parents are coming."

Andrew nodded. "They're trying to book a flight now but the airport in Oak City has been shut down because of the storms. They'll be here as soon as they can."

The surgeon nodded. "Okay then, folks. We have a plan." He hesitated, shook his head and walked away.

Paige turned to Zeke, her hand touching his face, and then reaching once more for his hand. Andrew found a chair for her, but she refused to sit. He finally shook his head and walked back to the waiting room, squinting at the clock. It was either really late or really early, he couldn't quite decide, seeing the clock read 4 a.m. Jason stood as he approached.

"Andrew?"

Andrew stopped, his eyes sliding closed for a moment. "It's not great, Jason. He's heading for surgery to stop internal bleeding. If he doesn't, the surgeon says he won't survive."

Jason shot a glance behind Andrew. "How's Paige?"

"Now that, I'm having trouble reading her and I never have had in the past. Our parents were friends, so I've known her all our lives. I just can't get a sense of what she's feeling right now." He sighed as he pulled out his phone. "It's Meg. Now I wonder what she wants. Meg? Paige? Yes she's here at the hospital with me. What's that? No, she's not hurt. It's Zeke. He'll be heading for surgery. Do I think you need to come? Not for a while. You are? Bring Gerry with you." He slid his phone back into its holster. "Meg's on her way in to be with Paige." He sighed. "I wish we could find these guys."

Jason nodded. "Me too. Are we any closer to finding them?

Andrew shook his head. "Not really. They've covered their tracks well. Bill is working full time on it for now but the trail is going cold. Even with the assault on Zeke, we don't know who it was or if it was even the same people."

Jason looked around, noting few people there. His eyes fixed on a small man standing just inside the doors, watching them. "Without being obvious, Andrew, do you know that man standing there by the doors?"

Andrew stretched, turning as he did so, his eyes glancing over the man Jason had spotted. "No. I don't but he looks familiar."

"That's what I thought, and I suspect if I go talk with him, he'll disappear."

"Not if he thinks you're leaving. You really do need to cut out of here, Jason. It's going to be a long time before Zeke's out of surgery."

Jason nodded. "I'll head out then and be back in a few. Call me if anything changes." He walked out past the man, who barely acknowledged his leaving with a flicker of an eye.

Andrew headed back towards Paige as he saw them wheeling Zeke out and towards the elevators. An arm around Paige to hold her upright, he led her to the elevator, not noticing that the man had followed them.

Chapter 12

$\mathcal{A}$ndrew tossed the paperwork he was reading back on his desk and scrubbed his hands down his face. He had left Paige under the guard of an officer while he had come in to deal with paperwork on his desk. He was getting nowhere with it. He looked up as Bill appeared in his doorway.

"Andrew? Did you get any sleep at all?"

Andrew shook his head. "None. I'm trying to work through all this and getting nowhere." He flipped his hand through some of the paperwork. "Where do we stand with Zeke?"

Bill sighed as he sat. "Nowhere, just like your paperwork. Nothing on his truck. No signs of anyone else there. The rain destroyed any evidence."

Andrew stared at Bill. "I think that was the plan, you know. Leave Zeke there to die. Going after him makes sense. He started it all when he went to Paige to look at her maps." He sat back, eyes thoughtful. "Find out who he talked to first, how he found out about Paige. Unfortunately, we can't talk to him. What about his friends?"

"I'll ask. I don't know if they'll be able to come up with anything though." Bill sat in silence, eyes staring at nothing. "It comes back to that map, doesn't it? The map that doesn't match the landscape anymore. What did Paige or Zeke see they shouldn't have?"

Andrew agreed. "There's something there, Bill. Now about that other fellow, the one who kidnapped Paige all those years ago? Anything on him?"

Bill shook his head as he stood. "Not a thing.   It's like he's disappeared from earth."

"That's what I was afraid you would say. Keep plugging away, Bill. Somewhere we'll find a crack and bust this wide open."

❂ ❂ ❂ ❂

Paige stirred in the waiting room, rousing from a light sleep she had fallen into. Jim stood in front of her as she sat up.

"Jim?"

Jim sat beside her. "Paige? How did we lose touch? You were one of my best friends growing up."

"Life, Jim. We both went our separate ways." She searched his faces, apprehension in her eyes. "Zeke?"

"They're just getting ready to take him to recovery. John said the surgery went as well as he could have expected. He's been able to stop the internal bleeding. Zeke lost his spleen but that's something a person can live without. What we have to watch for now is pneumonia, given his condition when he was found."

Paige nodded. "That's a real concern, isn't it? When can I see him?"

Jim sighed. "It's going to be a couple of hours anyway. Can I get you anything?"

She shook her head. "No, I'm fine. Have you heard from Zeke's people?"

Jim looked at her, then across the room. "They haven't been able to get out of their own airport yet. The storms just haven't stopped there. I spoke with his father a couple of hours ago. Here's their phone number. His mom would like to talk with you."

"I've never met them, you know." She stared at the slip of paper. "How do I call them and talk to them?"

"God will give you the words you need. There's a chapel just down the hall, Paige. It's empty right now. Take advantage of it. I can see you're still not at peace." He rose and walked away, Paige's startled eyes following him.

He's right, Lord. I still don't have that peace. It's eluded me for all my life. How do I find it? She rose and headed for the chapel, tucking the slip of paper into her jacket pocket. The officer followed her, taking up a position outside the chapel door.

Paige stared around at the plain room, counting the rows of pews, looking at the table with the cross on it at the front. She signed and slipped into the pew at the back of the room. Why, Lord? Why did Zeke get hurt? What was it we found that we shouldn't have? She crossed her arms on the pew back in front of her, sinking her forehead down on them. She sat, her mind wandering back over her life and the decisions she had made. Lord, where do I go from here? Is Zeke the one or not? I'm confused. I just don't get any of this.

Verses she had heard and memorized flitted through her mind, one after the other. She clung to the ones on peace. She needed that. She needed to find the peace with God and of God if she was to move forward. Events in the past few years had scared her and made her withdraw. She went through the motions but it wasn't enough anymore.

The door cracked open but Paige didn't hear it. She didn't hear Andrew enter and slip into the pew beside her. Finally sitting back, refreshed in her soul and spirit, she swiped at the tears on her face, startled with a handkerchief appeared in her line of sight. She stared at Andrew, then took it, wiping at her face.

"You okay?" Andrew's voice was quiet.

Paige nodded. "I can finally say I am, Andrew. I'm finally okay, after all these years. Why did it take that long?"

He shrugged. "You had to reach the point where God was all you had left. What happened to Zeke drove you to that point."

He sat, his eyes focused on the front of the chapel. "How's Zeke?"

"He was in recovery, I think Jim said, when I came here." She rose. "I need to go find out when I can see him. Have you talked to his parents? Jim had a while ago."

"I talked to his dad. They're finally able to fly out. I've sent Jim to meet them in Oak City. Your parents are opening up the cottage for them." Paige's parents had a little cottage on their property that they used for missionaries and those who needed it.

"I thought they would. Andrew, how close are you to finding these guys?"

Andrew shook his head as he waited for Paige to walk through the door. "No where near where we should be. They've gone into hiding, Paige. That worries me."

"Was it the ones after the maps or that other guy?"

"We don't know for sure but we think the ones after the maps. We can't prove that, though."

Paige looked up as she heard footsteps and stopped. How did he find her? She reached for Andrew's hand, and he pulled her behind him.

"What are you doing here?" Paige's voice was barely above a whisper.

"To find you, my dear. It's time you came with me." The man tried to brush by Andrew, but a hand to his chest stopped him. "Out of my way. Paige and I are leaving." He felt his arm grabbed and he felt handcuffs on his wrists. "What is the meaning of this?"

"For starters, assault, kidnapping, forgery. We have you, Steven Hart. Paige has told us what you did. I suspect she's not the first one or the last one. We're digging into your movements." He nodded to the officer standing behind Steven. "Take him down town, Bob. Book him. Then call Bill."

Paige leaned her head against Andrew's back. "Is this it for him? Is that really over?"

Andrew nodded, then turned to face Paige, his hands on her arms. "It is, Paige. He's facing more charges in other towns, including attempted murder and when they can prove it, murder. God kept you safe,

Paige. You likely would have been dead if you hadn't gotten away from him."

Paige shuddered. "That's horrible. At least one thing is solved." She looked past him to see Jim walking her way. "Jim?"

He smiled. "It's okay, Paige. Zeke's in a room in ICU now. I was coming to find you. Andrew?"

"Just a police matter, Jim. Come one, Paige, let's get you to your fellow." An arm around his friend's shoulders, he led her after Jim towards Zeke.

Paige stood, hand to her mouth, tears in her eyes, watching Zeke as he lay, motionless, in the ICU room. Her eyes once more traced the lines running from machines into his body, the monitors beeping and clicking. The nurse moved silently around the bed, finally making notations on the chart, and walking out of the room. Paige moved closer, her hand cupping Zeke's cheek.

"Oh, Zeke! Who did this to you?" Paige swiped angrily at the tears on her face. "Come back to me, please."

She finally found a chair, pulling it close to the bed, and sinking down into it, her eyes on Zeke. She knew now what they had meant when they said Zeke had crossed the line from friendship to something more. She had with Zeke. She wanted him in her live, God willing, for as long as they lived.

Chapter 13

Zeke watched as his mother moved around his hospital room, sorting through the flowers he had received, pulling the cards and putting them in a tidy pile. She finally turned, her eyes meeting her son's.

"Mom?" Zeke's voice held a question.

She smiled and moved to stand beside his bed. "You're being released tomorrow?" At his nod, she sighed. "And I have to head home today. I wish I could stay."

Zeke shook his head. "You need to get back to work. I'm on the road to recovery, as they say. Paige's parents are taking me in. I'll be fine."

"I know you will, Zeke, but you're still my baby and always will be. I just want to take care of you."

Zeke nodded, a smile in place. That was his mother, trying to make everything better, even though he was an adult and had been on his own for years. "Thanks, Mom."

"Where's Paige?   I haven't seen enough of that girl." She looked towards the door.

"She's working, Mom.   She has to. She had clients booked for the last few days and then she's going to have to go out in the field to do what she does."

"I don't like that, Zeke. Who's going with her?"

Zeke started to laugh.   "Mom, stop worrying. My friends are picking that up for me, as is Jason, Bill and Andrew. They're watching out for her."

"And who's watching out for you?" His mother stared at him, concern on her face. "This wasn't an accident, Zeke."

"I know, Mom. We have no idea who it was."

"You're keeping something from me, I can tell."

Zeke shook his head.   "Not really, Mom. We really don't know who it was."

"You need to come home soon, Zeke, for a visit, and bring Paige with you. She's special to you, isn't she?"

Zeke stared past his mom, his eyes unfocused as he pondered her words. Finally, looking at his mom, he nodded. "She's the princess you wove into the tales you told me when I was a boy."

His mom dropped a kiss on his forehead, studying the fading bruises. "She is that, Zeke, that and much more than your Dad and I ever prayed for you. She's the other half of your heart, son."

Zeke nodded, then looked past his mom as the door slowly opened, and Paige stood there, hesitant in her manners.

"Paige, come in, dear." Zeke's mom reached to draw her into a hug, then stood, her arm around Paige. "Zeke tells me he's heading to your parents' place tomorrow. I wish I could stay."

"I wish you could too. Mom and Dad have enjoyed having you to visit with."

Zeke watched the two woman who were so important in his life. How long,

Lord, before I pop that question? Is today too soon?

His mother finally left, Josiah arriving to take her to her plane. Zeke had mixed feelings about her going, but he watched as Paige said goodbye to her. He nodded. His two ladies liked each other, that was a given. He reached for her hand and pulled her to a seat on the bed beside him.

"Zeke! You can't do this!" Paige tried to rise, but he wrapped an arm around her.

"I can and I will! Just stay put, okay?" He grinned at the look of outrage on her face. "Listen, we need to talk."

She twisted in his arms. "We do?" A question lit her eyes and softening came to her face. "About what?"

"About you and me and where we go from here. Andrew tells me you were surprised that I had listed you as next of kin."

She nodded. "I was. Why?"

"Why? Why I'd do that?" At her nod, he bit his lip, hesitant to continued. "Because that's how I see you, Paige, as my lady, my next of kin, the one I want to spend the rest of my life with. I love you, sweetheart, in a way I didn't think I would ever love anyone." He watched as tears now sparkled in her eyes. "Aw, I made you cry. I didn't mean to."

She shook her head, her curls swinging with the motion. He reached to touch them, his hand gentle. "I never thought I would have anyone in my life, not ever, Zeke. After what I went through, I was scared. Too scared to let anyone close."

"We know that, sweetheart. It took quite a bit to reach your heart. I don't want to rush you."

She snuggled down beside him, her head on his shoulder. "You haven't. God has prepared both of us for each other. When you were in recovery, I spent time in the chapel, just me and God. I haven't done that in so long, Zeke. I felt like I had finally come home."

Zeke's arm tightened and he reached for her free hand. "I'm glad, sweetheart. Now, you know we need to make plans. That is, if you really do love me, and I'm waiting to hear that."

She laughed softly, then nodded. "I do love you, Zeke. I think I did the first time I looked up and saw you standing there in my office, so protective, so ready to jump right in and fight for me. You were so strong and so gentle at the same time."

"Can you reach into that drawer beside you and pull out the bag in there?" He took it and then tightened his arm around her again. "Paige, this isn't how I wanted to do this. I wanted a fancy dinner, you and me dressed up to the nines, soft music, the timing right, flowers, the whole romantic thing." He dumped a small box from the bag and opened it. He heard her gasp as she studied the ruby on the ring. "Will you marry me?"

She nodded, finally able to speak. "I will." She broke from their kiss, her eyes studying his face. "Why a ruby?"

"Proverbs 31, sweetheart." At her puzzled look, he continued, "Where it asks who can find a wife of noble character and that she is worth far more than rubies. That's what you are."

A knock at the door interrupted them. Bill poked his head in, his eyes taking in the two of them.

"Zeke, you look like the cat that got the cream."

"I did, Bill. I asked and she said yes."

Bill stopped at the foot of the bed, trying for a moment to figure out what Zeke was talking about. Then comprehension dawned.

"Congratulations, I think. This really isn't the most romantic place to ask, now is it?"

The two facing him laughed, and Paige slid from the bed, coming to stand near Bill.

"I have to run, but keep him in line, will you, Bill? I have no idea what he'll be up to next."

The two men watched her leave. Zeke turned to Bill, his eyes searching his friend's face.

"Give, Bill. Why are you here?"

Bill sighed. Zeke knew him too well. "We've tracked some of that contraband.

What did you get yourself mixed up in, Zeke?"

"What do you mean?"

Bill pulled up the chair and sat heavily. "That container they buried? It contains a new time of contaminant, one the environmentalists have never seen before. They're studying it thoroughly and analyzing it. From what we're told, it could really destroy the area it was released in, enough that all growth would be gone for years."

Zeke stared at him. "I had no idea. Who are these guys?"

"We're trying to find that out now. Rumour has it that's why you were attacked and left there. They think you saw something you shouldn't have seen. Paige was also taken because they think she has knowledge of the area on her maps that show where they're secreting their containers. That's what our sources are saying, anyway."

"Wow! Who would have thought?" Zeke grew quiet, his face and eyes thoughtful. "I'm going to be laid up for at least another three weeks. How do we keep her safe?"

Bill shook his head. "It's not just Paige, Zeke. It's you too. We don't have the resources to provide round-the-clock protection."

"I know that, Bill, and Paige does too. We've talked about what would happen if it was the worst case scenario, and this sounds like it is. So, how do I keep her safe?"

Bill hesitated. "I know you've just become engaged. Marry her quickly, Zeke. That way you'll be together when you're not working. Andrew's having the patrol make a pass around your places more often as much as he can. If it comes to it, we may need to move you to a safe house."

Zeke snorted. "Paige will never go for that. I need to be out there as well. We're short in the office already as it is."

Bill held up a hand. "I know that, Zeke. You two need to work with us, please."

Zeke watched as Bill walked away, then moved to sit on the side of the bed, catching his breath as he did so. He was told he had just missed coming down with pneumonia, that he needed to take time to heal, but his heart told him he needed to be up and moving towards protecting his lady. Lord, I'm still so weak.   I need Your strength.

Chapter 14

Zeke stood and watched as Paige moved around the backyard at her parents' place. He had been there three weeks and was due to return home the next day. Only for him, home was no longer a place away from Paige. He walked towards her, purpose in his steps. A few minutes of quiet conversation and then, hand in hand, they walked back to the house, looking for her parents and a phone.

Paige's Mom looked first at Zeke, then at Paige. "Are you sure, Paige?" At her daughter's nod, she wrapped her into a hug. "Then, we've got some planning to do. Zeke, here. Call your folks. Meg, go find your father. Paige, come with me."

Paige followed her mother to the attic, where she pulled out a trunk. "I've been saving this for one of you girls. You're about the same size as I was when your Dad and I married. It would be an honour, Paige, if you would wear it." She pulled out her own wedding dress, wrapped in tissue, turned creamy from age. She ran her hand along the material. "I look at it a few months ago, just to make sure it was still okay." She held it out to her daughter, tears in her eyes. "Paige, you are a beautiful, wonderful young woman. Zeke understands your heart, who you are. In life, it's not always that way. Your Dad did with me, from the very beginning."

Paige took the dress, then reached to hug her mother. "Thank you, Mom. Your blessing means so much."

Paige's mom stood. "All right, let's get you into that and see what needs to be done. What about a veil?"

"Is yours there?" When her mom shook her head, she sighed. "Okay. Let's just get some daisies then."

"You and your daisies."

❄ ❄ ❄ ❄

Zeke stood the next day in the backyard, Jonah at his side, waiting for Paige to walk towards him. They were still in danger, he knew, but he didn't want to lose a moment with the woman he loved more than his own life.

Later, as they drove away from the house Paige had grown up in, he turned to her. "Any regrets?"

She shook her head. "None whatsoever. You?"

He grinned as he reached for her hand. "None."

They had planned on being away for a week but returned before then, anxious to set up their new home. Zeke turned as Paige walked towards where he stood looking out the living room window and wrapped her into a hug.

"Did you find spots for everything I brought?"

She nodded. "I did. You really didn't have much, did you?"

He shook his head. "Not really. The furniture will go to a good cause, through the local mission. I had no real sentiment attached to it. I've been so busy working, I really didn't collect stuff."

She laughed. "I can see that. To tell you the truth, neither have I. I guess moving around didn't help, did it? Meg's been after me for years to add decorations and whatnot. I just didn't want to. Not until now." She turned, grabbing at his hand. "We need to go get groceries. You know - fruit, veggies, fresh meat?"

Zeke grabbed her back for a hug and kiss. "I can see I'm a henpecked husband already."

She hugged him close. "Not a chance, Zeke. You'll never be that."

Paige turned as a knock came to the door. "Who knows we're back?"

"I have no idea." Zeke peeked out the side window and saw nothing. Cautiously opening the door, he looked down at the flower arrangement sitting there. He frowned, reaching for the card.

Paige watched as he shut the door behind him, handing her the card.

"It's addressed to you."

Paige hesitated.   "Who would be sending me flowers like that? Any florist would wait for us to answer."

"I know. I don't like that." Zeke had his phone out, calling the police department.

"Let me have that. We'll let the police open it." Arm around her, he drew her to the kitchen, shoving her into a chair, and turning to brew a cup of tea for her.

Paige looked up at the knock at her back door, and then Andrew and Jason entered, their faces grim.

"Andrew?" Paige's face whitened more than it was already.

Zeke handed Andrew the card. "We haven't opened it yet. We left that for you."

Andrew took it, his eyes on the two. "When did you two get back?"

"This morning." Zeke stood with his hands on Paige's shoulders.

Andrew studied the small envelope and then pulled the card out carefully. He read it, his face growing stern. He handed it to Zeke.

Paige watched as Zeke read it, reaching for it.

Deepest condolences. Too bad you're not alive to see the grief.

"Who would send that?" Paige was white, the card dropping from her hands.

"That's what we need to find out, Paige. Is there anyone at all you can think of, either one of you, who would do this?"

"The only one I know of you've arrested. Is he still in jail?"

Andrew shook his head. "He made bail and was released yesterday. One of his conditions is that he stay away from you."

"Well, either he isn't or there's someone else." She picked up the card again. "It doesn't say who this is addressed to. And there's no name on the back of the card to say which florist it's from."

"We'll be looking into them all, Paige."

"And if it's not one from town, then what?"

Andrew finally walked away, not getting anymore information than he already had. Zeke followed him to the door.

"Be very careful, Zeke. I don't need to tell you that."

"No. No you don't. Do you think it was him?"

Andrew shrugged. "Who knows at this point? I can pretty much guarantee trying to track down the flowers is a dead end. Paige has that figured out."

Zeke nodded. "She has. How do I keep her safe?"

"That's what we'll have to work on. We also need to keep you safe, Zeke. You wander around all over the place, by yourself. How do we keep you safe? You're back to work on Monday, aren't you, and will be back out in your truck, following the weather systems."

Zeke agreed. "We'll do what we can, Andrew. Thanks for stopping by."

❂ ❂ ❂ ❂

Meg came running through the office one morning two weeks later, looking for her sister.

"Paige?"

"Right here, Meg. What's up?" Paige raised her head from her work to stare at her sister. When did she grow up, she wondered? She's not a little girl anymore, is she? I need to remember that when I'm talking with her.

142

Meg was frantic. "Paige. Who sent that vase of flowers in the waiting room?"

"What vase of flowers?" Paige rose and headed that way, Meg on her heels.

"That vase? It doesn't have a card. I already looked."

Paige walked close to look, then turned to Meg. "Call the police, please, Meg, and then leave. It's almost identical to one I had delivered to the house."

"The house?" Meg's voice rose. "You didn't tell us that!"

"No, we didn't. Now, do what I ask, Meg." She turned, hand on Meg's arm, and pulled her through the building to the back door. "Come on, Meg. Out we go. The dispatcher said there was a cruiser on its way."

"Paige, what is this all about?"

Paige shrugged, eyes on the building. "I have no idea, Meg. Neither do the police." She pulled out her phone. "I need to call Zeke and let him know what's going on."

Zeke stared at the sky and felt excitement building once more inside him.

A storm was brewing and he hadn't seen one like that in a while. He turned in a circle, camera up to take photos. He turned once more in the circle, eyes narrowed. Then he headed back to his truck, eyes watchful, not wanting a repeat of a few weeks ago. Once was enough.

Stopping at his office, he headed for his desk and computer, eager to download what he had taken. Sitting back as the download went through, he pulled out his phone. Paige had been trying to reach him, he saw. I'll call her in a minute, he thought, as he watched the photos emerging on his desktop. A fellow meteorologist stopped in and soon Zeke was deep in a discussion, forgetting his thought to phone Paige.

An hour later, he stood, catching up his camera and phone. His eyes slid closed. Paige! He had meant to call her. He needed to do better. They were a couple, a team now, and he needed to remember he had someone depending on him. He ran for his truck, heading for her building, knowing he was thirty minutes away.

"Paige? Sweetheart, I'm so sorry. What happened?"

Paige dampened down her frustration and anger. She knew Zeke had a tendency to forget what was happening around him when a storm moved through. "I got another vase of flowers, this time at the office. No card though."

"Has Andrew or Jason been there?"

Paige's voice faded for a moment. "They're here now, going over everything." She sighed. "How big is your storm?"

"It's massive, Paige, but it's not as important as you are. I'll be there in twenty, or less."

"Don't get a speeding ticket, okay?"

Zeke threw his truck in park and flew from it, anxious to find Paige. Jason pointed to the back of the building, and Zeke ran that way, finding Paige standing with Meg and Bill. Paige turned as she heard running footsteps and was enveloped in Zeke's arms, finally feeling safe that day.

"Bill, what do we have?" Zeke's voice was tight, his anxiety showing.

"Another vase of flowers. Funeral flowers in fact. No card. No note. Nothing. Nothing to tell us where they came from."

"Almost like the last time. Nothing on the security cameras?"

Bill shook his head. "Whoever it was made sure to keep their head down so their cap concealed their face." He turned as a patrol officer approached, handing him a sheaf of papers. "What do we have here?"

Paige moved to look at the photos. "It's him. I thought he was to stay away from me."

Bill nodded. "That's one of his bail conditions. We'll need to find him. Paige, we need you two to be very careful."

Zeke watched as the officers walked away, his arms tight around his wife. "Paige, what are we going to do?"

She shrugged. "I have no idea, Zeke. It's just getting worse. First him and now those other guys. Speaking of them, where are they in all this?"

Zeke nodded. "I know. That worries me. I don't think they've left town. I can feel someone watching me some days."

Meg spoke up. "I have no idea what all you two are mixed up in, but it doesn't sound like fun. What happens now?"

"Now we lock up and go home. I'll have to be in by 9 tomorrow. We have those clients coming in. Go on, Meg. You and Gerry have plans for the night."

They watched Meg walk back to the building and enter.

Chapter 15

Zeke turned as he heard Paige walking towards him, her socked feet soft on the floor. He drew her into his embrace, his head going down on hers.

"What are we going to do, Zeke? We can't pack up and move. I'm tired of running."

"I know you are. Come, let's sit and try and figure this out." Zeke drew her down onto the couch, arms tight around her. "Now, we go back over what we know and what you can tell me about this guy. Him first. Then we work on the other guys."

Paige nodded. Their conversation quiet, Zeke finally reached for a pad of paper and a pen, making notes, jotting down anything and everything they could think of.

Paige finally sighed. "What now, Zeke? I'm sure Andrew and Bill have all this."

"I'm sure they do too. Do you have the pictures of that area?"

She thought for a moment, then nodded, rising to go find her laptop. "I downloaded them to my laptop. Meg wiped them off the computer at work."

"Speaking of Meg, how serious is Gerry?"

Paige turned to study his face. "I have no idea. Why?"

"He asked my advice on a ring for her. I told him to talk to you, but he said he wanted a male perspective first."

Paige sat back, a thoughtful look on her face. "They make a really cute couple. She grounds him and he makes her come alive in a way I've never seen. When was he planning on springing the question?"

"He has great plans for Saturday night - flowers, dinner, you know."

She nodded, then searched through the photos on the laptop. "Here. Is this the one you wanted?"

He reached for the laptop, his eyes watchful. "It is." He studied it. "I need to enlarge it. How does your program work?"

She reached for the laptop, enlarging the picture for him, watching as he took it back.

"There. Do you see that?" He pointed to an area just at the edge of the picture. "Someone's standing there, watching us."

Paige shuddered, her hand going to Zeke's shoulder. "Who is that?"

"I have no idea. We need to print this. No, wait. Let me save it and I'll forward it on to Bill or Andrew. They can take a look at it." He sighed as his phone chimed an alert. "There's weather moving in. I was hoping it wouldn't tonight."

"That means you have to work?"

"No. Not tonight. Someone else is on call. They'll only call me if someone needs the time off or there's a huge storm moving in."

"That's good." She reached for her phone. "That's strange. I don't have my personal cell linked anywhere with work. So why am I getting a call from a client?" Scared, she looked at Zeke.

Zeke took her phone, watching her face as he did so. "No, you don't. I had to wait to get that from you." He looked at the number on the phone, then reached for her laptop. "Let me see if I can trace it." He searched. "No luck. How do you know it's a client?"

"I've had that call come into work and I've actually spoken with him." She rose and paced. "Zeke! It's him. Going back over our conversation, he never wanted to come into the office, only talk over the phone. With my job, that's not acceptable."

Zeke stood, reached for her hand, pocketing their phones as he did so. "Grab a jacket or sweater. We're heading down to see if Bill or Andrew are around. We need them to try and trace this number."

Zeke and Paige turned as Bill walked towards them.

"Sorry, Paige. We can't trace it."

Paige nodded, wrapping her arms around herself. "That's what I thought you'd say. So, where is he?"

Bill shared a look with Zeke. "We're tracking him, Paige. We can't be sure it's him, though." Paige stared at him. "Did you recognize the voice when you spoke to him?"

She shook her head. "Not really, but it always sounded muffled."

Bill drew a breath in, then spoke. "You need to be very careful, you two. No going off on your own to investigate. Got that?"

Zeke nodded, then reached to shake Bill's hand. "Thank you, Bill, for trying." He paused. "What about the email with the photo?"

"Now that's interesting, Zeke. No one else picked up on that. How did you?"

Zeke shrugged. "I don't have a clue. God, I guess."

Bill nodded. "We're working on that now, too. Take care you two."

❂ ❂ ❂ ❂

The next morning, Zeke walked Paige into her office, eyes scanning the area. He couldn't see anyone but he knew they were being watched. He had that feeling all the time now and didn't like it. He reached for the key to unlock the door and was surprised to find the door open.

"Didn't we lock up last night, Paige?"

"We did." She sighed. "Call it in, Zeke. They'll soon tire of hearing this address."

Paige walked through the office, Zeke at her side. She stopped at the room where the maps were kept and pointed. "There. The maps are moved around. I think….the ones from the forest are missing, Zeke. Someone got them."

"Paige, we need to take a trip back out there, without letting anyone know we're heading that way." He looked around. "I don't have to work on Saturday. Let's plan on that."

She nodded. "Zeke, how do we know the office isn't bugged by them, listening in on us?"

"I'll talk to Bill and see if they can search it for us. I've had the same feeling."

✿ ✿ ✿ ✿

Saturday found Zeke and Paige wandering back up the same path they had fled down not that many weeks ago. What would they find this time? Zeke had made sure Bill and Jason and some of his friends knew where they were going and had given them a time he would check in by. Paige stopped, listening, her head turning.

"It's so peaceful here, Zeke. I sometimes wish I lived out in the forest, away from the bustle of city life."

Zeke turned to watch her face, seeing the peace shining on it. "It would be nice. How be we look for an acreage or a cabin that comes up for sale and fix it up as our getaway?"

"I'd like that." She stopped once more. "I would love to be able to name the birds from their songs."

Zeke stopped at the edge of the forest, his eyes seeking the trees and undergrowth around them. "I don't like this, Paige. Someone's out there."

"You feel it too, don't you?" She shivered and not from cold. "How long will it take for you to search out the area you're looking at?"

"Not long. I just want to get some new photos and see if anything else has been disturbed." He turned to her. "Are there any other areas that you can think of similar to this that may be compromised?"

She shook her head. "This is the only one I've ever worked on. There are likely more areas, but it's not my work."

Zeke searched the area, not finding anything much different from what he remembered. "Paige, are there other areas in close proximity to these? Ones like this?"

She stood, lost in thought, then turned, eyes narrowing. "If we go back on the trail, we'll find another animal path that will take us over to a similar ridge. Do you think…?" Her voice died away.

Zeke nodded, a grim look in his eyes. "I do, sweetheart. I really do. Let's go."

An hour later, Zeke once more stood at the edge of the forest, his hand holding Paige's as they both stared. The earth was dug up, destroying the beauty nature had created. Zeke sighed. Another call to Bill or Andrew was in the works, he knew.

Paige dropped her backpack and reaching inside, pulled out her camera. "We need to take photos, Zeke. No one would believe us otherwise." She walked forward,

Zeke following, his eyes studying the area around them

"Take as many as you can. I don't want us here too long."

She nodded, then paused as she stared down. "This is different, Zeke. They didn't bury anything here. It's dug up and I can see the containers.   But why is this different? Why didn't they bury them?"

Zeke stared at her, then at the ground, suddenly reaching for her hand and pulling her away. He grabbed their backpacks and then strode rapidly down the path, coming to a sudden halt.   He looked around, then shoved Paige into the brush and down, pulling the branches back around them.

"Zeke?" A finger on her lips stopped her speech and she looked with wide eyes towards the trail they had just left. Men's voices carried to them.

Zeke reached for her camera.   A simple adjustment silenced the shutter sound and the flash. He raised it, clicking rapidly as the men passed, carrying containers he knew held the contaminants.

A sudden shout from behind them let him know their tracks had been spotted. Now what, he thought? Lord, where's your protection?

Zeke's hand on her shoulder kept Paige still. Neither wanted to give away their hiding place. How long would they need to stay here?

Zeke turned the camera to video, hoping to record the voices coming clear to them. Who were they?

Finally, the men left. Zeke held Paige back, waiting for what he wasn't sure. Finally, he parted the branches so she could make her way back to the path. He handed her the backpack she had been wearing. He pointed back the way they had come, needing to go back and see what the men had been up to. She nodded, and gripping his hand, walked forward. They stopped, eyes widening as they realized how many containers were now buried there, the tops just visible.

"Zeke, what are they planning?"

"I don't know, but we need to get to Andrew or Bill. They need to work with the proper authorities on this one. It's out of our league."

He turned to study her face, white now with fear and fatigue. "We'll likely need you to fly over and take more images of areas like this. Do you have someone you can trust?"

She shrugged. "I don't know anymore. Do you?"

"I might. Let me make some calls and talk to Andrew. Let's go. I'd like to find another way back to the truck, if I can." He stopped and groaned. "I just hope they didn't park in the same area as us. If they've been following us, they'll know my truck."

◎ ◎ ◎ ◎

Andrew looked up as Bill called out his name. He had disappeared from the office, hoping for a bit of quiet time. He sighed, looking down at his meal. Why, Lord, why do I never get to enjoy a meal without interruption? He was getting tired of being on call, of being the one who had to be it all to the officers and the public. Maybe it was time he retired. Lord, lead me in these decisions.

158

"Bill?"

Bill slid into a chair across from Andrew and waved the waitress over, placing an order. He pointed at Andrew's meal.

"Eat. You never take time when you're working to eat. You need to."

"Since when did you become my mother?"

"She talked to me. She's worried about you."

"Yeah, I know she is. You're looking for me for a reason."

"Not until we eat. So tell me, when are you moving to town?"

"What do you mean?"

"I know you've been offered the chief position. I'm praying for you."

Andrew sat, fork in hand, staring at his friend, then lifted the fork to his mouth. Chewing slowly, he swallowed his mouthful before he replied.

"I have been, Bill, but nothing's definite. It's a big step, one I'm not sure I'm ready for." His eyes grew distant. "I just wish things had been different."

Bill frowned, not sure what Andrew was talking about. "What do you mean, Andrew?"

Andrew shook his head. "Nothing, Bill. Just some thought running through my head." He looked up and nodded at the waitress standing there with the coffee pot in her hand. "Thanks, Suzy. How's the little one today?"

"He's better, thanks for asking, Lieutenant. The doctor said it was just a virus."

"Glad to hear that. Jimmy's found work?"

"He has. Thank you for the recommendation. He's quite happy there and they're glad to get someone with his experience."

"Good. Glad to hear that."

Bill sat back and watched the interaction. Whether he realizes it or not, he thought, Andrew has become part of this community. He's ready to take on that next step. I'll miss him on the county force.

Andrew finally sat back, eyes on Bill. "Okay, spill. Why'd you track me down?"

"Zeke and Paige are on their way in. They went back to the site in the forest and then found another one. They just missed being caught by the men. Zeke says he got some pictures and some video of them talking."

"A break? That would be nice, but I wouldn't count on it. Those men are not the head one and that's who we need." Andrew rose, throwing down some money to cover their meal. "Let's head back to the office, Bill. By the way, I hear a job offer as detective on the town force is heading your way."

Chapter 16

Zeke paced Andrew's office, waiting for him to return, a cup of coffee clenched in his hands. Things were getting out of hand, he thought. How did he go back to his work, searching out thunderstorms and worse, when a storm of unknown magnitude was brewing in his own life? He turned to watch Paige, sitting composed in the chair, a cup of tea in her hand. He saw the whiteness of her face, the grip she had on the cup, and knew how much she was terrified. He sat in the chair beside her, reaching for her hand. Her fingers curled around his, seeking warmth and strength from him.

Andrew stood in the doorway for a moment, watching his two friends. Paige was scared, he could tell, and trying hard to cover the fact. She had good reason to be scared. Bill had tracked down some of the men in the photos. Crime family members and their henchman. That made sense, given what the two had found.

"Zeke. Paige. What did you two go and do now?" Their heads shot up at his voice. He sank into the chair behind his desk, arms laid on the desktop. "Why did you go back out there?"

Zeke shrugged. "I just wanted to see what had been changed. It's my nature, Andrew. I look for things like that."

Andrew nodded. "And now they know you've been out there, right?"

Paige shared a look with Zeke, then spoke. "We don't know that for sure, Andrew. What we do know is that there are more and more containers out there. When are they planning to release that contaminant? And when they do, how do we fight it?"

Andrew sat back, sighing. "You're right. They're likely waiting for the right time. The right weather. What way would the wind have to be and how strong, Zeke?"

Zeke's eyes slid closed. That had been what he was afraid of. "That's how they plan to do that, isn't it? Wait for a big windstorm, without the rain."

"More than likely. It's only a matter of time. I've talked to your boss, Zeke. As of now, you're on our payroll. You'll be watching for just such that. You'll be sworn in as an officer for the time being."

Zeke stared at him, shaking his head. "I can't, Andrew."

"Why not? You'll not be armed. Your boss has been told what we've found. He wants you to work with us. Paige, we need you to go back over the maps you have on the area around us. I've made arrangements for a man from a friend's security team to provide pilot a plane for you. Ian Galbraith is a trained pilot and a security personnel. He'll be in on Monday to work with you on this, weather being suitable."

She nodded, knowing they had to do this. "You're right, once again, Andrew. We need to fight this, and this is the only way to do it." She looked at Zeke. "Zeke, you know that. God has led us this far. He'll led us on to where we need to be."

Zeke studied his wife's face, seeing the peace there, peace he didn't have himself. Lord, what are we getting ourselves into? Please, Lord, isn't there another way? If not, please send your peace to me, the peace Paige has found. Thank you.

His eyes slid closed as he pictured the forest and where the containers were planted. "Someone knows what they're doing, Andrew." He looked at him. "They've planted the containers where a good wind will pick up the contaminant and spread it over a good portion of the county. Have you had a ransom demand yet?"

Andrew sat back, surprised. "No, we haven't. That's surprising, isn't it? When do they send that out?"

"I would say likely within six to twelve hours of the wind picking up." Zeke rose, pacing once more. "We need to be prepared. Do they know what the contaminant is and do they have something to counteract it?"

Andrew shook his head. "They're getting close. They know what it is. It's just getting enough of a substance to counterbalance it. We'll post men out there once we know the timing better."

"Trouble is, Andrew, that could be weeks away. Do we have that long? What happens if the containers leak?"

Andrew stared at Zeke. "That's what we're looking at, Zeke. If we can identify the men and find the one in charge, then we'd be able to move in and clean up the areas, providing we can find all of them."

Paige stood. "Let us know when your pilot's ready to go up. Have him talk to Murray at the airport. He knows what I need. Unless it's not safe to do even that?"

Andrew shook his head. "Not likely. Ian'll be able to figure it out. Now go home you two. Relax for the next couple of days. I have a feeling it's the only relaxation any of us will get."

Andrew watched them walk away, then sighed, his head going down into his hands. Lord, where do we go? I feel so lost right now, not sure where we're going. I know you're in control, that you have a purpose for us out there somewhere. Guide our steps in this. Keep each of us safe.

He reached into his pocket, pulling out his wallet, digging deep into it. He pulled out the photo, faded now, creased, taken, he thought, fifteen years ago, just when he had joined the force. He rubbed his thumb across it, thoughts faraway from where he sat. He finally stuffed it deep into his wallet and returned his wallet to his pocket. There were things he needed to do. Wallowing in the past wouldn't help.

❂ ❂ ❂ ❂

Paige snuggled down beside Zeke as he placed an arm around her. She was tired but Zeke had felt they needed to be at church Sunday morning. She knew he was right. They needed this day to recharge themselves, to refresh for the battle ahead. She listened as their pastor spoke about peace, God's peace, and how to find it. *Lord, I need that peace. It's coming back to me, but I'm still not where I need to be. Help me, Lord, to find it.*

Zeke wrapped his hand around hers as they walked back to his truck. He watched as he helped her into the vehicle, then walked around to his door. Sliding inside, he started the truck, then waited.

"Zeke?" Paige's voice was quiet, but questioning.

"Yeah, Paige?"

167

"Why are we still sitting here?   I thought we were leaving."

"We are. I just don't know where to go today.   I feel like if we go to your parents, we're placing them in danger."

She nodded. "I agree. So where do we go?"

"How be we stop for some sandwiches or something and go walk by the lake?"

She smiled. "I like that idea."

Zeke drove away, his eyes watchful. Later, he took Paige's hand as they walked along the edge of the lake, laughing at the antics of the small children playing in the waves.

As they stopped, Paige leaned her head on Zeke's arm, her face pensive.

"What are you thinking about so hard, sweetheart?"

Paige shrugged. "Just life. I never thought I would ever marry, you know. I was resigned to living a single life."

"God had other plans for us, didn't he?"   Zeke tilted his head to watch the emotions flitting across her face. "You're scared, aren't you?"

"I am, Zeke. Just when I think I've found that peace God offers, something comes up that shakes me to the core."

"I know what you mean."

"But you seem so at peace in all this, Zeke. How?"

He shrugged as he tugged her with him to walk back towards the truck. "I guess I see the storms around me all the time and know that God can calm the storms for me within and without. It's just how I see Him."

Paige thought about that, then sighed. "I'm getting there, but nowhere close to where you are. Do you think those men will be back around this week?"

Zeke shrugged. "I have no idea. I know I feel someone watching us all the time."

Paige nodded. "I get that to." She stopped walking, eyes focused on their truck. "Who's that waiting by your truck, Zeke?"

Zeke stared at the man, then grinned. "I think it's your pilot, Paige. I've met Ian in the past when we worked a disaster together. Come on. Let me introduce you."

Zeke reached for Ian's hand. "Ian. Good to see you again. Glad you were free."

Ian grinned at Zeke. "It has been a while. And this must be Paige?"

"It is. Paige, this is Ian Galbraith. He works on a security team based out of Riverville. His boss and Andrew are friends." Zeke looked around. "Ian, are you staying overnight or coming back in the morning?"

"I'll fly in tomorrow morning, if you two can meet me at the airport by 6. But first, Paige needs to show me her maps so I have an idea of what she's looking for."

"Did Lydia come with you?"

Ian grinned again. "She did. She's waiting in my truck. Shall we?"

Paige watched as Ian walked back to his vehicle, then turned her eyes on Zeke as he helped her into the truck. "Security?"

Zeke nodded as he slid behind the wheel and then pulled out, Ian behind him. "He's on a security team, like I said. I'm just glad he was free to come help. He'll see things that we don't see."

Paige turned to look out the rear window, then looked ahead. "How did it get so complicated, Zeke?"

"I have no idea."

Later that day, Ian and Lydia stood at the door of the office, idly chatting with Zeke and Paige. Ian excused himself and walked away around the building, Zeke on his heels.

"Ian?"

Ian looked back at Zeke. "Zeke, has anyone gone over the building from a security standpoint?"

"Other than the police, no."

Ian nodded. "I thought that. Listen, Paige said her sister would be here tomorrow? Then let Joseph, our security system expert, come through here and at your place. Andrew's asked for that."

"Not a problem. Meg has a key to our house. Are you thinking someone placed something to watch us?"

"It's a given that they would, Zeke. Now about tomorrow. I'll land about 6. Tell me, is the weather to be good?"

"It should be. No storms. Maybe some clouds and light wind."

Ian nodded. "Good. Then we should be set."

❁ ❁ ❁ ❁

The next morning, Paige seated herself in the front of the plane, watching as Ian went through his pre-flight check. Zeke had fastened himself into the seat behind her.

Ian pointed at the headphones and Paige set hers in place.

"We're all set then, Paige?" At her nod, he continued. "Direct me to where you want to go. I don't think it will take long. You're comfortable working the cameras?'

Zeke watched out the window as Ian flew them back and forth across the areas Paige had indicated, praying that the men didn't see them or had no idea what they were up to.

Once back on land, Paige took the memory cards from the cameras, then turn to Ian.

"I can't thank you enough, Ian, for coming over to help."

Ian shrugged, a ready grin on his face. "It's what we do, Paige. It's ingrained in us to help. Now, don't be strangers."

Zeke and Paige stood back as they watched Ian fly away, then Paige looked down at her hands.

"I need to get to the office, Zeke, and you need to get to yours as well."

He wrapped an arm around her shoulder as they headed to the truck. "Not today, sweetheart. I'm on the police payroll, remember? I get to spend the day with you."

Paige stopped. "I had forgotten that, Zeke. Too much on my mind I guess. So now what? Will anything show?"

"I think there will be. I noticed there were more places that seemed disturbed and not from nature."

Paige sighed. "That's what I was afraid of. Let's go and get these loaded.

Then I want to store these cards at the bank."

"Good idea." Zeke stood, hand on the closed truck door, looking around. He could feel evil near him, but where was it coming from? He turned in a circle, eyes watchful, then glanced at the sky. Clouds were moving in, he thought, in more than one way.

Chapter 17

Zeke stood behind Paige, watching as she flipped through the photos she had uploaded and then compared them to the maps she had spread out.

"Right there, Zeke. There's another area that's been disturbed."

"I see that. How many is that we've found?"

"Too many. It's all in the same area, just difference clearings. Who is doing this?"

"I wish I knew." Zeke blew out a breath. Just what is going on, he thought? Andrew hasn't shared much other than to ask I keep a watch on the winds. What kind of chemical is being used and how dangerous it is?

Paige pulled him over. "Look, Zeke. What is that?"

Zeke stared at the picture. "That's not a container buried. What is the exact location?" He reached for his phone. "Bill? Paige and I are going over the photos from this morning. We have one that looks strange. No, I don't think it's a container. The area is too big. That's what I'm afraid of. Sure, we'll be here for a while." He tucked his phone back into his pocket. "Bill's heading our way."

"Zeke? What aren't you telling me?"

Zeke sighed and then crouched down beside Paige, an arm going around her. "It looks more like a grave, Paige, than a container."

"A grave?" Paige stared at the photo. "How do you get that?"

"The size for one thing. Bill will be able to tell more."

Bill stared at the photo Paige had on her computer screen. "Can you enlarge that area for me, Paige? Thanks." He leaned closer. "Definitely not the containers. It's what you were thinking, Zeke. It looks like a grave. We'll need to get up there. What is the location, Paige?"

She jotted it down and handed it to him along with the photos she had printed. "Here. If you need anything else, let me know."

Paige turned to Zeke. "Now what?"

Zeke shrugged. "We need to let them do their job. Come on, sweetheart. Pack it in for the day and I'll take you stargazing."

"Stargazing, huh?" She grinned. "Now that sounds like fun." She reached to hug him. "Meg's already gone for the day, so it won't take long."

Zeke watched as Paige laid back on the blanket he had spread out near the lake, her eyes fastened on the sky.

"It's been a long time since I've done this, since I was a kid. Thank you, Zeke."

He nodded, his eyes not leaving her face. "You're welcome. We need to do this more often, sweetheart."

She turned her head to watch him. "We do." She studied his face as he reached to kiss her. "We need to find things to do as a couple."

Andrew looked up two days later as Bill appeared in his doorway, his heart sinking at the look on Bill's face.

"What do you have, Bill?"

Bill handed him a medical report. "From that grave on the ridge."

Andrew shot him a look, then read through the report. "We don't have a name yet?"

"We're working on it. The medical examiner thinks the man was homeless, just going by his clothing, but we're not just looking at them. He's being very careful in examining him, taking precautions. He thinks it was the contaminant that killed the man."

"The contaminant? They tried it out on him." Andrew sat back, eyes on his desk top. "That makes sick sense, you know."

"We need to find these guys, Andrew. If they even suspect Paige has taken more photos, they'll be after her."

Andrew nodded. "And I have no idea how to find them or even how to keep Paige and Zeke safe. They won't lock themselves away, I know."

Bill turned as he heard footsteps approaching. Great. Zeke is here and we're no further ahead in our investigation.

"Bill. Andrew. I needed to bring this to you." He held up a package. "This was left on our doorstep sometime overnight. We've checked our security cameras. Whoever it was kept to the shadows."

Bill took it and set it on a cleared spot on Andrew's desk as the two men shared a look.

"I'll call a tech in." Andrew reached for his phone. "There was nothing on the tapes?"

Zeke shook his head. "Just a dark shadow. The timing was around 2 o'clock."

"That's in-between the times the patrol car was by. Whoever it is seems to have upped the ante, don't they?"

The three men watched as the tech cleared the package for them to open and then cut the paper and then the tape holding the box closed.

Andrew nodded his thanks, then with gloves on hands, opened the box, a puzzled look on his face.

"What's in it, Andrew?"   Zeke watched Andrew's face.

"It's really bizarre. There a bouquet of roses, Zeke, as well as a card."   Andrew drew out the card and pulled it from the envelope. His face grew stern as he handed it to Bill.

"Andrew? Bill?" Zeke was worried, his eyes sliding between the two men.

"This is not good, Zeke. It's another direct threat at you two."

Zeke reached for the card, his eyes dropping to read the words.

Give us the photos or you die. Twenty-four hours.

"What photos?" Zeke had a feeling he knew.

"Somehow they figured out that you took more photos. They're watching you two very closely. We need to go back through your house and Paige's building."

Zeke nodded, knowing Paige was not going to like it, not one bit. "Ian said his friend Joseph would be around today to go over our security systems."

"Joseph?" Andrew shot a look at Bill. "Is he there now?"

"He was to be."

"Bill, head over there with Zeke. Ask Joseph to check out everything. He's more experienced at that than we are."

Zeke stood leaning against Paige's desk, his eyes on her. She refused to look at him, telling him something was wrong. He finally drew her to her feet and into a hug.

"Talk to me, Paige. Tell me what you're thinking."

"I thinking I have to close this place down, once again, and move."

"Not happening, Paige. Not this time. We're not moving anywhere. This decision doesn't just affect you anymore."

She sighed as she wrapped her arms around him. "When did life become so difficult? Where's the fun we're supposed to be having?"

Zeke dropped a kiss on her hair. "It will come, sweetheart. Joseph's gone to go over our home. Bill's with him. We have an officer stationed in the waiting room. Meg's gone home to be safe."

She nodded. "I know. I just want this over, Zeke. I want to go on with our lives and we can't."

He stood back to see her face, his hands on her arms. "We will."

She leaned against him once more. "Zeke, are we going to have to go into hiding?"

He sighed. "We have made to. Andrew's talking that way."

"I don't want to. I want to face this guy and get it all over with."

"The thing of it is, Paige, is that we have two different people. We know who one is, but not the other."

"Paige? Zeke?" Bill's voice proceeded him down the hall. "Joseph's done his work. He's made some recommendations that you really don't need to follow, seeing as you already have good security. But that's not stopping these guys."

Zeke looked at Bill over Paige's head. "I can hear what you're going to say. Paige doesn't want to go, you know?"

Bill nodded. "We may have no choice soon, guys. Whoever this is has upped their threats." He turned to look at the front of the office. "Joseph found some listening devices planted here in the office. None in your home."

"So that's how they knew?"

Bill nodded. "We need a tech to go over your computers, Paige, to make sure a program hasn't been uploaded to them."

Paige turned to him. "So does that mean we have to disappear?"

Bill nodded. "Andrew would like you to, until we can track down these guys. We're getting close, Paige. We identified the lower level and are working through the men you saw in the forest. We've made some arrests." He pulled out his phone as it chimed, a grim look coming over his face. "That body we found out there? That was your stalker, Paige. I had no idea."

"He's dead?" She sank into her chair. "How did they get to him?"

Bill shrugged. "That's what we'll be investigating, Paige. Now, about you two. Where do we put you?"

Zeke stared at Bill for a moment. "I have a conference I need to be at. Paige comes with me and learns how her maps help us out."

"That's a good plan. Do it." Bill turned to walk away. "Let us know your agenda and when you leave and return. We'll be struggling away here, trying to make sense of it all."

Paige's voice stopped him.

"What name?" Bill's face whitened as she repeated it. "Are you sure, Paige? That changes it all, now doesn't it?"

Chapter 18

Paige turned in her seat, staring around at the auditorium they were seated in.

"I didn't realize it would be so big a conference, Zeke."

He grinned. "We gather from all over the country and even some from other countries. This is one of our biggest conferences. I'm glad you can share it with me this year." He pointed at her program. "See, your work affects us. Without you and your fellow cartographers, we would have great difficulty in knowing exactly where the storms have hit."

She sat back, eyes on his face. "That's really important, isn't it? I never thought of it that way before."

"It is. You don't realize how much your work means to other professions and just the public in general. You work in the background. We take what you do and use it in our work." Zeke sat back as the opening speaker approached the microphone. "Thanks for coming."

She leaned against him. "Like I had a choice?"

He shook his head even as he smirked. "You had a choice. You chose to come with me."

At the end of the day, Zeke grasped Paige's hand and led her towards the dining room.   Nodding at friends and acquaintances, he seated her at a table, then sat beside her.

"So, what did you think?"

She stared at him. "I'm not quite sure what to think. That's a lot to take in."

He nodded. "It is. There is always new information coming out. This is just one way we deal with it." He looked around. "Do you have conferences like this?"

She shook her head. "Not really. I suppose there might be but I never go." She shivered as she looked around. "I feel someone watching us, Zeke, just like at home."

Zeke stared her. "Someone here?" He sighed. "I do too. That means whoever is after us works as a meteorologist somewhere close to where we live. I'll need to talk to Andrew or Bill."

"Later, Zeke. Let's enjoy the time with your friends and colleagues. If whoever we suspect is here they can't really harm us, can they?"

Zeke nodded even as he turned to speak with someone, the thought niggling at the back of his mind that whoever was after them was there, watching their every more.

❂ ❂ ❂ ❂

Four days later, Zeke carried their bags into the house and to the bedroom as Paige headed for the kitchen. She needed that cup of tea she had been craving for the last few hours. The weather had turned extremely hot and muggy. Zeke had warned her that bad weather was coming, but she had shrugged it off.

Zeke stood at the kitchen doorway, watching Paige as she moved around the room. She was scared, Zeke knew, and

187

trying hard to cover it. When, Lord, when do we have peace in this? When does it end?

"Zeke?" Paige stood staring at him. "Do you want tea or coffee?"

"Whatever you're having is fine, Paige." He reached to pull her into his arms, tightening them around her. "We'll get through this, sweetheart."

She nodded. "I know we will. I just want it over. Did you talk to Andrew yet?"

"Not yet. I thought I'd call him in the morning. Tonight, we need just to spend time with us. I love you, sweetheart."

She sighed, relaxing against him. "I love you too, Zeke." She stopped, her eyes tracing the room. "Something's off in here, Zeke. Was the security system disturbed at all?"

"No, it wasn't. What do you see that's off?"

She shrugged. "I'm not sure. Just a feeling that stuff has been moved and put back. Nothing I can put my finger on."

"Let's check the rest of the house." Holding her hand, they walked through the house, checking out each room, then headed for the back door. Looking around outside, Zeke frowned. "I don't see anything moved out here, but I agree. Someone has been around."

Paige clung tighter to his hand. "It's them, isn't it, Zeke? They knew we were away and tried to find what they wanted."

He nodded. "Has Meg said anything about the office?"

She shook her head. "Everything's fine there. Gerry's been with her as much as he could."

"I'll call Andrew or Bill in the morning. Now, do we have any food in the house? Any popcorn or something like that?"

She stared at him. "Popcorn?"

He grinned. "Sure. We need to watch a movie so I can cuddle with my girl. We need popcorn to watch the movie."

She shook her head as she moved towards the house. "Zeke, you're crazy."

"That's right. I'm crazy about you. So, do we have popcorn?"

❂ ❂ ❂ ❂

Bill looked up from his reports when he heard his name called.

"Zeke. When did you two get back?"

"Last night. Listen, Paige thinks someone has been in the house."

"In the house? But you have security in place. Wasn't it upgraded?"

"It was." Zeke sank into one of the chairs in the office. "I've looked at the tapes and checked the security log. Nothing shows but I trust what Paige feels."

"That's bizarre. I'll have one of our techs take a look at it." Bill sat back. "That's not the only reason you're here."

Zeke stared at his friend, gathering his thoughts. "Paige mentioned something at the conference. She could feel someone watching us, just like here."

Bill sat forward, arms on the desktop. "At the conference? Oh, man, does that mean we have a meteorologist involved?'

Zeke nodded. "I suspect we do. That's why they want the maps. They need to update their system so they can properly bury the canisters to do the most damage.

They need to know where the wind will blow."

Bill sighed. "You just don't stop, do you? Every time we talk, you have something else to add to the mix. But I think you're right. There's more involved than just this. What I can't figure out is why there hasn't been a ransom demand of some kind."

"There won't be, will there? They'll just release the chemical, whatever it is, when we have a big storm. They're building up to something big, Bill. This is just a test for them."

Bill nodded. "We need to replace those containers and we're working on that. We just don't know how many there are or how they plan to release the chemical."

"Likely by remote. They're not going to be standing there and release each one."

Bill agreed. "That's what we think. Listen, how do we keep you two safe? If they've been in your house, they're still looking for information."

"I know they are. I just don't know what they're looking for. We haven't kept anything, turning everything over to you."

"We know that. But they seem convinced something is still out there."

Zeke stood. "I'm heading out for a while. I need to look over my equipment and make sure it's ready for the next big storm. Weather is changing, Bill. The humidity and heat are building to a bad storm."

"Pray that this isn't the one they've been waiting for."

Zeke stood, staring at his friend. "What do you mean?"

"What are they waiting for? We've had some good winds lately. If that's what they wanted, why haven't the released the chemical?"

"They need the right time of year, that's what. When would a contaminant do the most harm? Spring, summer or in the fall when everything is going dormant. If the chemical is released when things are dormant, it would be released again when spring comes and do a whole lot more damage if it attaches to any pollen in the air."

Bill sat back, his face whitening. "I think you're right, Zeke. Oh man, what have we gotten involved in?"

"I pray that you find all the containers and get them replaced. Keep me updated."

Bill watched Zeke walk away, then, sighing, stood himself to go find Andrew.

Chapter 19

Andrew walked towards Zeke and Paige after church on Sunday, as they stood in the parking lot talking with friends. He didn't like to disturb them, but things had happened overnight and he needed to move them to somewhere safe. He waited until they were alone, then spoke.

"Zeke. Paige."

They turned as they heard his voice, Paige's hand seeking Zeke.

"Andrew?" Zeke was puzzled, not quite sure what Andre wanted.

"We need to talk, you two. It's time to put you both somewhere safe."

"What do you mean?"

Andrew pointed at Zeke's truck. "Get in and follow me. We're going back to the department and talk."

Paige stared at Andrew as he walked back to his vehicle. "Really? Just like that?"

"Come on, Paige. We need to at least go and talk with him." Zeke tugged her with him to his truck. "It's the only thing we can do. He must have new information or something."

"I like that 'or something', Zeke. What more can happen?"

He shrugged as he followed Andrew through town. "Who knows."

Andrew watched as Zeke and Paige sat in front of him, eyes hooded, his thoughts going to what he needed to say. He sighed to himself. They wouldn't like it, he knew. Not one bit.

"Andrew? What's going on?" Paige spoke.

"Paige. Zeke. Every time I think we have an answer, something more crops up. Your suggestion of a meteorologist was spot on, Paige. We've arrested one of your former colleagues, Zeke, a Rick Thurston."

"Rick? Somehow, that doesn't surprise me. He was always a little too over the edge."

"He's talking but not providing names. He may not know who hired him, but we're searching through everything we can on him. The one thing he did mention was that you two were to be taken out. You know too much." Andrew sat back, his eyes watchful. "That means we need to put you two somewhere safe."

Zeke sighed. "That won't work, Andrew. You know that as well as I do. You don't have the manpower to do that."

Andrew nodded. "I know we don't. That's why I'm bringing in a team of security experts. Don and his crew will be here later this afternoon. He's set up a place to hide you two for the next few days."

"And if that doesn't work, then what? How long do we have to hide for?" Paige was not happy. "I have work I'm committed to. I can't leave it. People depend on me to provide these maps and photos."

"We realize that, Paige. We're trying to figure out a way you can continue to work."

Paige stood. "Let me make it clear, Andrew. I'm not running. I'm not hiding. Zeke can do what he wants, but I'm staying in town." She walked out of the office and away from the two men.

Zeke stared after her. "What she said, Andrew." He too walked away.

Andrew watched them walk away, his hands running through his hair. Okay, that went well. Now what?

Don poked his head in the door. "Went about how you thought?"

Andrew nodded. "It did. They're running from us, Don. Now what?"

Don leaned against the doorway, a thoughtful look on his face. "I know you want to keep them safe and hide them away. With their occupations, you can't do that. So we leave them here in town and my guys stay with them."

"Will that work?"

Don shrugged. "Any better suggestion? They're newlyweds. They're not going to accept someone living in their home. And I wouldn't either. We put men outside during the night and keep someone with them during the day."

"That's what we'll have to do, then, I guess. Set it up. Here's Zeke's cell number. You get to call him this time."

Don laughed. "It won't be the first time we've been fought on something like this, nor the last. Let me see what I can do. If I can handle this, it will free you up to follow your investigation."

"That it will. Thanks again, Don. And good luck."

Don walked away, eyes thoughtful. Now what, he thought? How do we do this?

❂ ❂ ❂ ❂

Zeke pulled the house door open, surprised to see Bill standing there.

"Bill? What are you doing here?"

"Can I come in, Zeke?" At Zeke's nod, he stepped inside. "Andrew has a friend coming to talk to you two. Please listen to him. We need you to be safe and staying on your own means you won't be."

A sudden scream from Paige had Zeke running her way, out the back door and down the yard, Bill on his heels.

Zeke caught Paige in his arms, her hands outstretched.

"Paige? What happened?"

"I don't know. My hands are hurting, Zeke. All I did was reach for the stepping stone there."

Zeke scanned her hands. "They're burnt, sweetheart. Bill?"

Bill had already called for paramedics and then the crime scene team.

"Let's get Paige looked after. Go with her, Zeke."

Zeke watched as the paramedic treated Paige's hands, then looked up at him.

"I have no idea what we're dealing with here. I need to transport her."

Zeke nodded. "I'm with her. There is no way she's going on her own."

Bill watched them walk away, then turned as a tech approached. "What do you have?"

"It's some sort of chemical, Bill. What, I'm not too sure."

Bill sighed. "You know that chemical you've tracked down? Compare that to it and see if you can come up with a treatment for it. I'll alert the Emergency physician as well."

Zeke watched, his eyes on his wife's face, as the physician treated her hands.

"It's a chemical burn, Paige. We need to keep you here for a while. Treatment isn't something you can do at home. We'll be admitting you to a floor."

She sighed, pain evident on her face. "That would be too easy, now wouldn't it? All right. Zeke stays with me."

The physician grinned at her. "I didn't think he would be going anywhere. By the way, there's an officer in the hallway. Andrew tells me you're now under police protection. I don't want to know why, but I think it's a good idea. I'll be back in a few minutes."

Zeke moved to sit beside Paige on the stretcher, his arm going around her. "Lean on me, Paige."

She leant against him, her head on his shoulder. "Who would do that, Zeke?"

"Andrew must be getting close to whoever it is. This is a warning, Paige. We need to take every precaution we can." He sighed. "I think we'll have to go away, as much as we don't want to. You'll not be working for a while."

She shook her head, pain bringing tears to her eyes. "I won't be. This is so frustrating, Zeke." She looked up as Andrew appeared in the doorway, a man with him she didn't know.

"How are the hands, Paige?"

"Sore. How would you expect them to be?"

Andrew watched as she blinked back tears, knowing that she would soon be put on an IV for pain management and treatment.

"Zeke, Paige. This is Don. He's here to look after you both. He has a security team he's moving into place for the next while."

"A security team, Andrew?"

"Yes, Zeke, a security team. You both will do what he says. If you don't, I'll stick you in a jail cell. Which would you prefer?" Andrew walked out of the room, leaving

Zeke staring after him and Paige staring at Don, a puzzled look on her face.

"Have we met before, Don?"

Don shook his head. "Not that I know of, Paige. Now when are you being admitted?"

Paige sighed. "They're working on that now. Go, talk to the physician, and find out what room I'll be in. Zeke's staying, so don't even think of separating us." She looked past him. "Mom, Dad?"

Her parents entered, staring at first Don, then Paige.

"Paige?" Her mother's voice held a question.

"I don't know who did this, Mom. All I know is that I picked up something in my garden that should have been safe and wasn't."

Her father stared at Zeke, then at Paige. "Care to explain why it was contaminated?"

"We have no idea, Dad. Andrew and Bill are working on it." She looked past him as the physician entered. "Look, guys. They want to get me to a room. You two and Meg really need to stay away from us for now. Please!"

Her parents stared at her, then at Zeke. At Zeke's nod, they said their goodbyes and left. Don stood near the door, his stance relaxed, but his eyes watchful and alert as Paige was settled back on the stretcher and then wheeled from the room, Zeke keeping pace with her.

Zeke stood at the closed door, eyes watching it, waiting until Paige had been settled into her bed and the IV started. Don stood near him.

"Don? What's your plan?"

Don turned to Zeke, noting one of his men standing nearby. "I put one of my men at the door and one down near the elevator. Two of us are with you at all times. We have a list of who is or isn't allowed in. Anyone who goes in has to have been cleared by me. That means nurses, physicians, aides, lab techs, cleaning staff. No one goes in without it. Your friends will want to come and see her. Keep them away. Phone calls are fine. No texting. No computer, although Paige won't be doing that for a while."

Zeke nodded. "I get that, Don." He ran his hand through his hair, then rubbed his neck. "I have no idea how long she'll be in for."

"A few days from what I understand. The burns could have been a lot worse. We'll make sure your food is safe as well. You won't be eating hospital food. One of us will do a food run for you."

"That sounds good." Zeke looked up as the door opened again, and he entered.

Paige was sleeping by this time, the pain medication and sedatives kicking in. He stood, hand on her cheek, watching as she slept. *Why, Lord? Why Paige? She's struggling to make sense of everything right now, to find Your peace, and then this happens.* He finally lowered himself to the bed beside her and gathered her into his arms, his eyes falling shut as he too slept.

Don stood in the doorway, watching for a few minutes, then closed the door. He nodded as his man stood at the door. He headed for the waiting room. There was work he needed to do and he also needed to talk to Andrew. What had they gotten involved in, he wondered? He looked up as he heard footsteps heading his way. Just the man he needed to talk to.

"Andrew."

"Don. They're settled?"

Don nodded. "Both are asleep. From what you've said, they've had a rough few weeks."

"That they have and it's not over, not by a long shot. Come on. Let's walk outside. I'll fill you in on as much as I'm able to."

Chapter 20

Zeke turned from the window in Paige's hospital room. It had been a long four days with her hands being treated. She was to be released that day, and he had no idea where they were heading. Don hadn't said when asked, nor had Andrew. *Let it be somewhere safe, Lord. I can't take much more of this and I know Paige can't either.*

"Zeke?"

He turned as Paige walked towards him.

"Did Don say anything?"

He shook his head. "No, he hasn't. I don't think he will until he has us settled somewhere."

She sighed. "I just want to go home." She wrapped her arms around Zeke. "I'm tired, Zeke, tired of all this."

"I know you are, sweetheart. Not being able to work won't help."

"Neither of us can. How does that affect yours?"

Zeke shrugged. "It does, but I told Andrew that if really severe weather moves in I have to be available. That's how it goes."

They turned as the door opened, and Don entered.

"You two ready to go?" At their nod, he continued, "You have your instructions and prescriptions, Paige?"

"I do. Someone will need to fill them for me."

Don reached for them. "Paul has volunteered to do just that. Now, let's get on the road."

Paige and Zeke followed him from the room and down the stairs to the back of the hospital where they were tucked into a large SUV.

Don slid in beside Paige and nodded at the driver. "Now, just a few rules. No computers. No phones. If someone needs to get in touch with you, they have been told to call Andrew. We're heading out of the city to a place we use every once in a while."

Zeke stared out the window, eyes narrowed. "How far out, Don?"

Don smiled. "Now, Zeke, don't ask. We've had your family go in and pack some gear for you two. Your cat, Paige, is at your sister's."

Paige drew a breath of relief. "Thank you. I was worried about her." She stared around her. "Don?"

"You know the area, don't you, Paige? We're not staying where you think we are."

Zeke studied the two, then turned to watch the two men in the front of the vehicle. "What can you tell us, Don?"

"You'll see where we'll be in about twenty minutes. We'll keep you here for as long as we can, but we may need to move you again. You need to turn off your phones and let us have them for now."

"Our phones?" Paige shook her head. "I need that to work."

"Meg is looking after that for you right now. Your clients have been advised that you're out sick and have all rescheduled.

Zeke, I've spoken with your boss. He will call me if he needs to."

Zeke shook his head. "How long, Don? How long do we keep our lives on hold?"

"Andrew and Bill are working through the evidence now. They haven't told me what they've found, but I got the impression that they had found something interesting." He pointed at the cabin the vehicle stopped in front of. "This is home for now. Let's get you inside and settled."

❂ ❂ ❂ ❂

Two days later, Bill went looking for Andrew. Not finding him, he let out a huff of frustration. He had information that he needed to run by him and how could he when Andrew wasn't around? He pulled out his phone as it chimed.

"Don?"

"Bill. I wanted to let you know we're moving them. Somehow, someone found us. We don't know how. We've been over everything we brought with us, any jewelry, keys etc."

"Don, do they have key fobs?"

Don didn't respond for a moment. "I know what you're thinking. Hold on."

Bill could hear quiet conversation in the background and wondered what Don was up to.

"Bill? That's how. Somehow or other a tracker was placed in Paige's key fob. We've take it out and searched Zeke's."

"Well, that's one less thing to worry about. Let me know if we can help in any way."

"Will do." Don was gone before Bill could add anything.

"Problems?" Andrew's voice startled him.

"Yeah. Don found a tracker in Paige's key fob."

"A tracker? Now, that's interesting. What else did he say.?"

"Not a whole lot, other than that they were moving Paige and Zeke."

Andrew sighed as he headed for the break room, nodding and speaking to various officers on the way. "Where do we stand with the investigation?"

"I was looking for you. I've had the team take over the one conference room and lay out everything. I pulled Jason in as he knows the areas around here better than I do."

"Good idea. There's a spot opening up in the detective pool again, Bill. Lee's moving on. Jason would be good. Make sure I get his application for it."

Bill nodded as he accepted the mug of coffee Andrew handed him. "I've been tracking Thurston's trail. He's way in debt from gambling."

"That's why he was snared into this. Has he talked at all?"

Bill shook his head. "Not one word. Whoever it is has him scared."

"That they do. Now, who is involved from the town?"

"That's what I would like to know. So far, I haven't found the connection yet."

Andrew pointed at the whiteboard as they entered the conference room. "Look for someone you would least expect, who has lots of hidden assets. Someone has to have a chemical background to develop this or have contact with someone who does."

Bill stopped, his mind going over the people in town. Then his eyes slid shut. "I know a couple, Andrew. Two at least that have the capability of this. But I don't know if they'd sell out."

"Run with it, Bill. Now, if you need me, I'm heading to a meeting with the town emergency team. Zeke was worried enough that he talked to some people and got the team started."

❂ ❂ ❂ ❂

Paige flipped through the magazine she was holding, nothing catching her fancy to read. She raised her eyes to watch Zeke, engrossed in a book.

"Zeke?"

He looked up, a smile on his face. "Bored?"

"I am. I don't like this."

"I know you don't, but your hands are not recovered enough for you to do a lot." He rose, his hand going out to her. "Come on. Let's see if we can at least go out on the patio for a while."

Don turned from where he had been watching the backyard of the house. Paige and Zeke watched him from the patio.

"Don, any word from Andrew?" Zeke's voice held hope.

"None, Zeke. I know they are working through it, but I haven't talked to Andrew in a couple of days."

Paige sighed. I just want this over and to go home."

"I know, Paige." Don looked down at his phone and then pulled it from its clip, walking away as he answered it.

Zeke pointed to the chairs on the patio. "Let's sit, Paige. At least we're out in the sun and fresh air."

She nodded. "Zeke, I feel like I've been missing something. I wish I could get on my computer. There was something about that one map that puzzled me."

He rose. "Andrew sent a copy with us. I'll get them." He returned and set the package in front her.

Paige pulled out the maps, her eyes focused on each one. She finally handed one to Zeke. "There. In the edge of it, what do you see?"

He looked. "I'm not seeing anything, Paige." He looked up at her.

"On the left. There a vehicle of some kind, isn't there?"

He looked again. "You're right. An ATV. Wait! There's someone standing behind it. How did we miss seeing that when we were taking those photos?"

Don stopped at the edge of the patio, listening to their conversation. "You found something else."

Paige nodded, handing him the photo and pointing out the area. "I know that man, but I can't put a name to him."

Don shot her a look, then studied the photo. "I know who it is. I think you've just found another link in the chain, Paige. He's a renegade chemist. The authorities have been looking for him for years."

He pulled out his phone and once more walked away, photo in his hand. Returning, he sat, his eyes on his phone before he shoved it back on its clip.

"I just spoke with Andrew. The man you found is wanted by multiple authorities. To have him here in our area is not what Andrew wanted to hear. We suspect he's behind this contaminant."

Paige shuddered. "That's what I thought. Now what, Don? How does that affect keeping us away from everyone?"

"We stay the course. Two of my men will head in with this photo. We'll be moving you two again tomorrow."

Paige sat back, a disgruntled look on her face. "Again? Don, how many times will we be moved?"

"As many as it takes. This time, we're taking you out of the Elmton area."

Paige threw up her hands. "I'm done." She rose and strode rapidly back into the cabin, anger sparking from her.

Zeke watched her go, then turned to Don, a hard look coming into his eyes. "What didn't you say, Don?"

"What do you mean?"

"Andrew's told you something that causing you to move us once again. And it has to do with that photo." Zeke pointed at the photo Don still held.

"He did, Zeke. Right now, he's still investigating an angle to the case. He's not saying anything until he knows more."

Zeke rose, staring down at him. "Let's hope he's not too late in telling us and we're dead by that point." His gaze went to the distance. "I know God's in control, Don, but it sure feels like He's forgotten us." He turned and walked after Paige.

Don watched him go, then stared at the photo once more. Lord, I have no idea which way this is going to go. We need to keep those two safe and I have no idea if we'll be successful. Let them feel Your peace today about all of this. He rose, heading to find the two men to send into Elmton.

⚛ ⚛ ⚛ ⚛

The chemist turned to the man who had hired him and cringed. The man was not happy, he could tell, and he just hoped he lived to see the next day.

"What do you mean, they've disappeared? Weren't they being watched? Weren't you tracking them?

216

"We were. Somehow our tracking devices aren't working anymore. They have just disappeared."

The leader's fist rose is anger and he stood over the fallen chemist. "If I didn't need you to finalize the release of it, you'd be dead. From now on, Len stays with you wherever you go. He has orders to kill."

The chemist dragged himself to his feet, fear coursing through his body. For the first time in his life, he had come across someone meaner and more dangerous than himself. He slouched from the room, Len on his heels.

The leader threw the glass he was holding towards the fireplace, the liquid flaring in the flames, glass shards scattering on the hearth. How did he ever get involved with such an idiot, he asked himself?

Chapter 21

$\mathscr{B}$ill looked up as Don's men approached him.

"Is that the photo?"

They nodded. A few words of conversation and they walked away, leaving Bill staring at the photo. He turned to find Andrew.

"Andrew? Here's the photo. It's worse than we thought."

"What do you mean?" Andrew studied Bill's face even as he reached for the photo.

"I know this man and I know who he's been working for." Bill stared at the wall behind Andrew. "How do people get so evil?"

Andrew didn't answer, just waited for Bill to speak. When Bill finally gave a name, Andrew's eyes slid shut.

"You're right, Bill. Much worse than we thought. All right. Gather your team. Lock yourselves in and get to work. Meals will be sent it. If you need to take a break, use the other board room. I don't want any of your team making personal calls, taking any personal calls or texts for the next forty-eight hours. Don's warned me that Zeke has said a storm is moving in. With the heat and humidity, he's expecting a bad one. We know what that means."

"That we do. Okay. Pray that we find the evidence before the storm hits. Are Zeke and Paige still safe?"

Andrew nodded. "For now. Don's planning on moving them right out of the area, but won't tell me where."

❂ ❂ ❂ ❂

Don hesitated before he climbed into the SUV beside Paige. Something was off, he could feel it. What it was, he had no idea. Taking one last look at the sky, he stopped, staring at the sickly green colouring. Ducking his head, he spoke.

"Zeke, what does that sky mean?"

Zeke stepped back out, his eyes raised. "I don't like it, Don. That usually means

219

tornadoes. We're overdue for one. The mugginess today feels like a really bad thunderstorm. My mom would say you could cut the air with a knife."

"That's what I was afraid you'd say. Let's get on the road and get you two situated once again."

Zeke stood, hands in pockets, staring around. "Will we be safe there, Don? I don't get why you keep moving us."

"We normally don't move as much, Zeke. But this is Paige's home area. We've had to keep her safe and away from her known haunts. Taking you out of the area will help. Now, in the vehicle. Let's go."

Zeke seated himself, shutting the door behind him, and reaching for Paige's hand. Her hand was cold and shaky.

"Paige?" Zeke tried to get her to look at him, but she refused. "Paige?"

"It's okay, Zeke. Just a feeling that it's all coming to a head and quickly. I hope it's over this week. I want my life back."

Don shared a look with the driver, then watched the young couple. He was a couple of years older than them but that day felt decades older. This was a time in every security detail that he hated, knowing the end was in sight but not knowing when they would be attacked once again. An attack was coming, he knew. It always did.

Zeke pulled the blanket up over Paige as she lay stretched out on the bed in the room they had been assigned. He gently changed the bandages on her hand. God had been gracious; the wounds were almost healed but he would keep the bandages on for another day or so. He brushed the hair back from her face, his thoughts in the future, wondering what their life would be like when they weren't on the run. God would be central, he knew, but what else would be there? He was blessed that Paige had agreed to marry him, but he still knew she had issues with peace and trust she had to deal with.

He turned, pulled the door closed behind him, and went to stand looking out the front window. Don had surprised them by bringing them to Oak City, to a rundown subdivision. He never expected that and he suspected Paige didn't either. Don seemed to know what he was doing, he thought. He turned as he heard footsteps behind him.

Don stood, his eyes on the window, then on Zeke, sighing as he knew he had to chase him away from there.

"We need you to stay away from the windows, Zeke. In fact, we need to close the drapes."

Zeke turned, surprise and protest on his face that died when he saw the look on Don's face.

"Still not safe, Don?"

Don shrugged. "Likely, but we take no chances." He pointed at the couch. "Sit. We need to talk."

Zeke sat, his eyes on his hands as he rubbed them together. He heard the faint sounds of thunder starting and the wind picking up.

"Your storm's moving in, Don."

Don agreed as he sat across from Zeke.

"Okay, Zeke. Here's where we lay it on the line for you. Andrew has Bill and his team holed up at the department, working non-stop to gather all the information and evidence they can. They know the name of the leader and the chemist. Thurston has finally talked as well. Andrew's hopeful they can get the warrants they need and arrest the men today. If not today, then tomorrow."

"But that doesn't solve the problem of how the contaminant will be released, does it?"

Don shook his head. "They've solved that and are working on a solution to prevent the release. He hasn't said what yet."

He looked over his shoulder as he heard one of his men moving around the house. "We'll do everything we can to keep you two safe."

Zeke's attention was drawn away from Don and towards the outdoors. He rose suddenly and almost ran to the window.

"Is there a basement, Don?"

Don nodded, on his feet and heading for the kitchen. "Paul, find everyone and hit the basement."

Zeke ran for the bedroom and scooped Paige into his arms, heading for the basement as well. "Over there, by that wall. Down and cover your heads as best you can."

They heard the thunder grow louder and could see the lightning strikes, the rain heavy. Then the sound of a freight train roared past. The house shook and they could hear tearing and breaking of the structure. After what seemed hours, there was quiet.

The men moved slowly, eyes on the floor above them.

"Was that what I think it was?" Paul spoke for the group.

"A tornado." Zeke looked down at Paige, who cuddled down in his arms, fear on her face. "It's over, Paige. The storm has gone."

Don headed for the stairs, two of his men at his heels. "The rest of you stay here. We need to check out what happened upstairs." He tried the door but it was blocked. He stared around. "Let's see if we can push it open, guys. Something's against it."

They finally managed to get the door open and Don headed through it, staring around at the destruction. Half the house was gone. His hand on his head, he spun in a circle, then headed for the outdoors. Just what he thought. The vehicles were destroyed. Now what, Lord?

He returned to the basement, struggling to come up with a solution.

"Half the house is gone. The vehicles are destroyed." He met the stunned gazes of those who had stayed in the basement.

"This is not good, Don." Paige struggled to her feet, Zeke's arm around her. "Zeke, this is not what I wanted to experience."

"I know, Paige, but we can't control what nature does." He stared around. "We stay here or try and walk out?"

"Our best bet is to walk out. Fortunately, we all have backpacks, not luggage. Let's go. It will be dark in a couple of hours and I'd like to be as far away from here as we can be. Hopefully we'll find a motel or hotel we can get rooms in."

They stared in shock at the destruction surrounding them, then headed out of the area. Don's men had grabbed their knapsacks as they ran for the basement.

Zeke and Paige's were gone, the bedroom side of the house being destroyed.

An hour into their walk, they stopped. Paige dropped down onto a park bench, Zeke wandering around near her. Paul stood behind her, eyes watchful, as Don and the rest of the team spread out. Don was trying to get through to Andrew but couldn't. He pocketed his phone with a sigh. It would be another hour at least before they reached the downtown area and safety, he hoped. He didn't like having those two out in the open, but there really wasn't a choice.

Sudden squealing of tires drew Don's attention, and then gunfire had them down the ground, their weapons out. A van careened into the park, blocking Don's view of Paige and Zeke. He could hear yells and then slamming doors before the van took off. He rose to his feet and ran for the bench.

Zeke was on the ground, not moving. Don looked around, and his heart sank. Paige was missing as was Paul. They had been found. He dropped to a knee beside Zeke as Zeke moved.

"Are you hurt, Zeke?"

Zeke shook his head as he sat up. "No, I don't think so. The van clipped me as it came past." He looked around, panic rising. "Where's Paige?"

"She's not here, Zeke. Neither is Paul."

Zeke stared at Don, then jumped to his feet, searching for his wife. "Where is she?"

"Someone got her, Zeke. Paul's with her."

Zeke dropped back to his knees, hands covering his face. "It's them, isn't it? How did they know?"

"I have no idea, Zeke. Only a few outside of our team knew where we were headed."

One of the team, Thomas, Zeke thought his name was, approached Don, an object in his hand.

"This is how they found us, Don. I have no idea how they got it on Paige."

Don reached for it. "A tracker on her necklace? I think we searched everything."

"We did."

Zeke reached for it. "That's not her necklace, but I did see her with it a few days ago. I have no idea where she got it from." He turned it over and over. "It looks like one of those promotional things. That's from the conference we were just at."

Don sighed, knowing Zeke was right. Phone out, he strode away to try to make a call, just as cruisers pulled up.

"Andrew? Don. Bad news. Paige has been taken. Yeah, I know. We went through it. We were heading back into town when a van separated us. Paul's with her. Yeah, we'll need transportation. Our vehicles are toast. Zeke? Not good. Okay. See you in a bit. The Oak City police are here. I'll send you an address where you can find us."

Hours later, Don found Zeke in a conference room at the Oak City Police department, head cradled on his arms. Pulling back a chair, Don sat, waiting for Zeke to respond.

"Any word, Don?" Zeke raised his head, his face bleak.

"Not yet. Thomas got a partial plate so they're running it."

"What are the chances they'll find it?"

Don shrugged. "Don't lose hope, Zeke. We'll find her. Now, were you hurt at all? I know you said you weren't."

Zeke shook his head. "Just some bruising. The paramedics didn't think it was enough for me to go to the hospital. Where do we go now, Don?"

"Home, Zeke. We're heading back to Elmton. That's where they'll take her. It all revolves around those areas you two found." He looked behind him as the door opened. "Andrew and Jason are here. Let's go."

Zeke didn't rise. "How do I tell her parents and Meg?"

"Andrew's spoken with them. We have all four tucked away somewhere safe for now."

Zeke rose, fatigue evident in every movement. "Pray you find them soon, Don. I've been talking with a friend. There are more tornadoes in the forecast."

Don nodded. "We'll find her Zeke. God will lead us to her."

Chapter 22

Paige sat up, hands reaching to pull off her blindfold. She blinked and stared around. Where was she? Panic and fear set in and she drew her knees up and wrapped her arms around them. It wasn't a house, she could tell.

Memories assailed her. The panic when she saw the van heading her way, the gunfire, not seeing Zeke, being shoved into the van and being bound and blindfolded. She knew someone else had landed in the van with her but who she wasn't sure. The men had not spoken one word, she realized. She stood finally, rubbing her hands up and down her arms. She didn't even know what day it was. The room was dim, dim enough she couldn't tell exactly what it was.

She stumbled and fell to her knees, the shock of landing on rock vibrating through her. She felt around, knowing she heard breathing.

"Zeke?" She felt along the body, finding the man's face. "Oh, Zeke, it's not you. Who?"

A groan greeted her and the man moved. "Paige?"

"Paul? It's you. Where's Zeke?"

"Help me sit up. They did a number on me." Paul leaned back on his hands, trying to orient himself. "Zeke's safe. They didn't get him, Paige. He's with Don."

"Where are we then?"

Paul shook his head, the movement barely visible in the dimness. "I have no idea, but I suspect we're in the forest somewhere outside Elmton. It's a cave or mine or something like that."

"We don't have any mines in the area, so it has to be a cave." Paige sat back, arms crossed against the chill. "There are caves just outside town." A chill not related to the dampness of the room went through her. "The caves are near one of the container sites."

Paul sighed, knowing this was true. "Have you seen or heard anyone?"

She shook her head. "I haven't been awake all that long. Do we have guards?" Her gaze shot towards the entrance.

"I would image we do." He felt along his belt. "They've taken my weapon. At least that one."

"What do you mean?"

Paul shook his head, then rose, heading towards the light. "Stay here, Paige. I want to see what's out there."

He stopped and backed up as he heard footsteps, standing in front of Paige. A small rotund man entered, followed by two others. The dimness made identification impossible.

"Well, Paige. I see you're up and on your feet. Good. We need to talk."

Paige stared at him. "Gary Brown? How did you get mixed up in this?"

"Money, Paige. I was offered a lot of money. That trumps anything else."

Paige shook her head, sorrow on her face. "Money doesn't buy your happiness, health or friends, Gary. Did you never learn from your dad?"

Paul listened intently the conversation, wondering how Paige knew their captor. His eyes traced between the two and then to the two men standing behind Gary. His eyes narrowing, he watched the older of the two, catching a slight head shake as he did so.

"Where I'm heading, it will. Leave my dad out of this. He was no good."

"You're following in his footsteps, Gary. Doing what he did, only a lot worse." Paige's head rocked sideways from the blow across her mouth.

Paul dove towards the man, landing awkwardly from the blow to his head and lying still. Paige's hands were at her mouth as she stared in horror at the men.

"You'll not be leaving here, Paige. Nor will he." He turned and walked away, followed by the two men.

Swiping her hand across her mouth, Paige dropped to her knees beside Paul, rolling him to his back.

"Paul?" Tears streaked down her face, tears of pain and fear.

Lord, how do we get out of this? I know You needed to get my attention, but there were easier ways. Zeke would tell me to pray for peace here, that You're in control. So that's what I'm doing.

She sank back to a sitting position, eyes on the entrance to the cave. There had to be a way to get both Paul and herself away from her. Her eyes turned to Paul, who was by now moving his head slightly. Just how badly he was hurt, she had no idea.

Hours passed, Paige sitting watching the entrance to the cave. Paul had roused and was by now pacing the area, eyes watchful, every once in a while rubbing his head where he had taken the blow. He had to get Paige out of there, he knew, but how? He could see the shadows at the cave entrance, showing dark against the setting sun.

❂ ❂ ❂ ❂

Andrew tracked down Zeke in his office, stretched out on the couch. He stood for a moment watching him sleep, then sank into the chair at his desk, his eyes on his paperwork. Might as well work on it, he thought, while we're waiting for news. He

234

hadn't heard anything yet, but he knew he had teams out looking. Off duty officers had volunteered as well as the search and rescue teams.

He finally sat back and stretched, his paperwork finished. His eyes searched the window. It was dark. He squinted at the clock. After midnight. And still no word. He rose, heading for the conference room to find his team.

He stood, searching the room, finally finding Bill. He walked towards him, stopping as he saw the whiteboard, then nodding. Good, he thought, progress.

Bill turned as Andrew stopped beside him, then pointed back towards the door. He stopped just outside, where he could still keep an eye on the work going on in the room.

"Where are we at, Bill?"

"We have the warrants and teams are getting ready to serve them. Jason's going to lead the one against Gary Brown. Once thing I can't figure out, though. I don't think Gary's our top guy."

"He's not. He's never had the smarts for that. A good chemist, which is why he got sucked into this for the money, more than likely." Andrew turned to look around. "Where is Don't team?"

"In the smaller boardroom. They refused to leave."

Andrew nodded. "Can't say as I blame them. I'll go talk with them. What else?"

Bill and Andrew spoke quietly for a few minutes before Andrew moved off. He stopped just inside the door of the boardroom, his eyes watching the men as they turned to the door, Don rising to his feet to come closer.

"Andrew? Any word yet?"

Andrew shook his head. "Not yet. My team's heading out shortly with the warrants. I'm praying we find something soon. Did you think of anything that would help?"

"Not really. We didn't get a plate number on that van, but Thomas got the impression it was a commercial van."

Andrew shot Thomas a look. "Why?"

"It had a series of numbers and letters on the back door and it was more a commercial-type van than a passenger van. It didn't have a name on it though."

Andrew sighed. "That goes with what we've found out. Thanks, Thomas. We'll keep you guys updated. Can I get you anything?"

Don shook his head. "Your people have done so much already. How's Zeke?"

"He was sleeping when I left my office." Andrew turned as he heard his name called.

Jason stood there. "We're ready to head out with the warrants. Bill waiting out back, but he had word there's bad weather moving in."

Andrew nodded. "That would be about right, now wouldn't it? Go on, Jason. Let me know if you need me for anything." He turned to head back for his office, Don watching as he moved away.

Zeke stirred, his hand going up to scrub across his face. He sat up, staring around, disoriented for the moment. Then, he pulled out his phone, the insistent chiming finally getting through to him.

His face paling, he rose, heading to find Andrew, almost running him down in the doorway.

"Zeke?" Andrew's hand went out to steady him.

"This isn't good, Andrew. There's a tornado warning out. It's to go right through the area when the containers are."

Andrew turned Zeke around and shoved him into a chair, closing the door behind him. He sat in the other chair, his eyes watching the fear rising in his friend.

"Zeke. What I am about to tell you can go no further." Andrew explained what he met, Zeke's eyes never leaving him.

"But where is Paige? And Paul?"

"That we don't know yet, Zeke. We're working on that. Bill and Jason have gone off to serve warrants. Come, let's get you with Don and his men. I was about to send out for food."

Zeke shook his head. "I'm not hungry, Andrew."

Andrew hauled Zeke to his feet and hand on his shoulder, directed him out the door. "I know Paige well enough to know she'd want you to eat something. There will be sandwiches coming in as well as some cold drinks. We have coffee or tea here."

Zeke stopped, hands clenching, eyes full of pain. "Do you think she's still alive, Andrew?"

"We have no reason to think otherwise, Zeke."

Zeke nodded, not moving for a moment, his heart raised in prayer for his wife and Paul. "I don't get it, Andrew. Why did they take her?"

"We're working on that too, Zeke. Come on. Get some food into you. Or at least something to drink." Andrew stood and watched as Zeke moved into the room, Don stopping him to talk to him, before he sighed and moved away. What he hadn't wanted to tell Zeke was what he was thinking, that Paige had been taken for revenge and she wouldn't be coming home, not yet and maybe not at all.

Paul watched through the dimness as the two men left to guard them moved restlessly. He could hear the occasional complaint from one of them, a young man he thought. The other one didn't say a lot. He desperately tried to come up with a plan to get Paige out of there, but with the men at the entrance, and no other exit, there wasn't much he could do.

He turned to search for Paige, his eyes finding her huddled up again the wall. He pulled off his jacket and draped it around her, shoving his hands into his pockets to try and keep them warm. She didn't move, her arms wrapped around her legs, cheek resting on her knees. He knew she was awake, he caught the odd flash of her eyes when a flash of lightning lit the night sky.

His eyes once more on the entrance, he stopped pacing. Something was up. He could hear raised voices and moved closer so he could hear better.

"Where are they? They were supposed to be here to relieve us before dark."

"They'll be here. Something likely came up." The voice of the older man, Paul thought around his own age, was calm, unlike the high-pitched excitement in the younger man's voice.

"I say we kill them and head out. They're not coming back."

"We do nothing until we hear from them. It won't be looked on kindly if you kill them and the boss comes back and needs them."

"I tell you. He's not coming back. We've been left holding the bag."

The voice died away. Paul frowned, trying to figure out what happened. He backed up as a form appeared in the entrance and watched as the older man dropped the younger man to the floor and straightened up, his weapon now drawn and pointed at Paul.

Chapter 23

*A*ndrew headed for the boardroom, on the prowl for both Zeke and Don. Bill and Jason were still working through their warrants, but Bill had gotten word to Andrew. He knew where they were holding Paige. He needed to get out there and he wanted Don's crew with him. With the officers serving the warrants, he would be short staffed. Tad was on his way in with Suzy and her search and rescue Border collie. Hopefully, they wouldn't need either one.

Don looked up and then reached over and touched Zeke's arm. Zeke was on his feet, dread in his face.

"Andrew?"

"It's okay, Zeke. We know where she is. Come on. Don, all of you too. I have Tad and Suzy on the way in. We'll need all of us to work together." He stopped. "Zeke, how bad are the storms to get and what track are they on?"

Zeke stopped, eyes on Andrew's face. "Find me a map and I'll show you."

Zeke's finger moved across the map Andrew had spread out on the table. "They're targeted to go right through here." His voice died away as he pulled out his phone. "The storms are moving in rapidly. Andrew, we won't have time to make it out there."

Andrew's heart dropped as he realized what Zeke was saying. "How long?"

"Thirty minutes max until they hit full force. It would take us that long to get out to the parking lot and then at least that long to climb to the first site." He spun and began pacing. "Would they have been able to find shelter?"

Andrew shook his head. "We have no idea, Zeke. All we can do is pray that they have. Can we move in there safely?"

Zeke shrugged. "Not likely. These storms have spawned tornadoes all along their track." He held up his phone. "The latest word is that the tornadoes are an EF-3 at the least."

Andrew's eyes slid closed. "Pray that they're somewhere safe, Zeke. As soon as the storms are through, or the worst of them, we move out. Let's work on getting our gear together so we can move out as soon as we can."

Don pulled Andrew aside for a quiet word before heading off with Thomas. The other three of men moved towards Andrew and Zeke, asking what they could do.

Tad stood for a moment, watching, then moved forward. "Andrew, what's the word?"

"We're just about done serving the arrest warrants and the search warrants. We have teams from here and Oak City moving in to search. The county force is involved as well. Where's your wife?"

"She's in your office with Beauty. She thought that would be the quietest place for now." Tad gave a cheeky grin.

Andrew laughed, the light moment refreshing. "Right now, it likely is. All the action seems to be away from here or right in this area. We'll need your expertise in helping set up the teams and search parameters."

"Do we know at all where they are?"

Andrew pulled Tad aside. "I haven't said anything to Zeke, but we've received word from an undercover officer. They're being held in a cave. The trouble is, it's right at one of the container sites."

"Now, that's not good news."

"No, it's not as bad as you think. We've taken steps with the containers."

Tad shot him a quick look, then stared past him at Zeke. "Does he know that?"

Andrew shook his head. "We've kept it as quiet as we can, only two officers, myself and now you're knowing that. I know how hard it is on him. We needed to make our arrests first."

Tad nodded. "I know the reason, but will he? He doesn't think like we do."

"I know, and that worries me. I hated to put him through this." Andrew turned as he heard hurried footsteps moving towards him. "Bill?"

"Brown got away. He wasn't there when we got to his house. His wife said he left about thirty minutes before we arrived. She thought he was heading out to the forest."

Andrew paled. "He found out somehow. Who's the leak?"

"That I intend to find out." Bill's voice and face were grim. "It wasn't one of our guys. I can guarantee you that."

"That changes everything, now doesn't it?" Andrew could feel the anger rising. "We now have to head out into those storms and pray we survive. Zeke! Don, good you're back! Let's roll! We've had word the mastermind is heading out to where Paige is being held."

Zeke paled. "Where?"

"There are some caves out that way, Zeke. I doubt you would have known. He has them stashed there."

◉ ◉ ◉ ◉

Paul moved back further into the cave, more towards Paige as he watched the man in front of him. Their eyes met. Then the man stooped and pulled the weapons from the younger man. He then turned to Paul.

"You don't know, and I know you don't know if you can trust me. You can." He held out the weapon, butt first, to Paul. "Take this. You'll need it. Brown's on his way back but I don't know if he'll make it before the storms strike."

"Brown?" Paul's voice held more than a question.

"Yeah. Brown. He's that short guy she knew. Everyone thinks he's the boss, but he's not. There's someone over him. I've been trying to find it out, but no one but Brown knows, if he even does."

"What's in this for you?" Paul spoke after a moment or two of silence.

"I can't tell you. Just trust me."

"You won't tell us, but you expect us to trust you. You've been standing out there preventing us from leaving and you want us to trust you."

The man nodded. "Please. Just trust me." He turned as Paige moved. "We need to get her out of here. When Brown returns, his orders are to kill her. I can't let that happen."

Paul studied him in the flashes of light, then finally nodded. "So, where do we go?"

"We need to move and move fast. Get her on her feet. I'm leaving this kid here. He'll make his way out when he wakes up."

Paul finally nodded, reaching to pull Paige to her feet. She didn't respond as he took her arm, her eyes blank, her face expressionless. Shut down and broken in spirit, he thought. She's prepared to die. Lord, help us. Lead us out of here and restore peace to Paige.

"Okay, which way?"

"Follow me. I know the storm picking up, but Brown won't care. He's too depraved to even value his own life. He'll make his way here. The good thing about the rain is that it covers our tracks. If we go to the left, about two miles away there's an old cabin. It will do for now, until we can make our move to get off this ridge."

Paul struggled to stay upright in the wind, his arm around Paige to keep her moving. He knew if he removed it, she would just drop where she was and not get up again. He stopped abruptly when the man did.

"Listen, I need to know what to call you. I can't just call you "Hey, you"."

The man laughed. "Call me Shane. That's good enough. How's she doing?" He nodded at Paige.

"Not great. We need to find somewhere soon." Paul wiped his arm across his face, trying to clear some of the rain from it.

"It's only about a half-mile now. We'll be able to get a fire started, I hope, and dry off. There may be some food. I know you two haven't eaten in a while."

"I'm fine but I would like to try and get something down Paige. She's giving up."

Shane nodded. "I know she is." He shrugged out of a jacket and wrapped it around Paul. "You can wear this for now." He shot a look behind him. "I don't think we're followed but we need to get moving."

Paul looked around as the wind picked up and he made a grab for Shane's jacket, shrugging into it and then wrapping an arm around Paige once more. "Let's move. I was through a tornado already this week. I don't want to go through another one."

"Let's hope we don't."

Shane finally pointed through the heavy rain and darkness. "It's right there. I found it one day when I was exploring. I doubt Brown or his cronies would know it was here."

Paul nodded as he followed Shane through the rickety door, shoving it closed behind him. He looked around, dismayed at the debris and dust in the room. He found the cleanest spot and eased Paige down to the floor. He crouched, watching her face, noting the blankness on it. He sighed. Lord, help. I can't do this. I need to get her back to Zeke and I don't know how we'll do that. He stood and walked around the room.

"I checked out the chimney last week when I was searching out this place. It's clear. We can get a fire going and then move her closer to the heat."

"Why were you searching out a place?" Paul stopped him with a hand to his arm.

"Because Brown had this plan to bring those two here, tie them up and leave them in the cave when he released that contaminant."

Paul's face whitened. "He wasn't, was he?" At Shane's nod, he swallowed hard. "He really is a piece of work."

"That he is. Here, I have some tea, no coffee, and some bottled water. I stashed it here last week, thinking I could try and get them away from him."

Paul reached for the water and looked for a pot. Finding one, he headed for the outdoors to rinse it out in the rain, bringing it back in and filling it some water before setting it near the fire. He held out his hands, the warmth feeling good. He roused Paige enough to move her closer to the fire and watched as she curled up on the floor, her eyes open and staring ahead.

Shane watched as well. "She really has given up, hasn't she?"

Paul nodded. "She has. I don't know her that well, but I would say this has taken a lot from her."

Shane walked to the door and back, his pacing stirring up dust and debris, before he stood back by Paige, watching her. "The storm will likely soon be over. Catch some sleep if you can, Paul. I'll stand guard."

"Wake me in two hours and I'll take over."

✿ ✿ ✿ ✿

Zeke shook his head, trying to clear the rain that was dripping from his hair onto his face. The rain gear they were fitted out with wasn't of much help, the wind whipping the rain around them in heavy sheets. He leaned closer to Andrew just to hear what he was saying.

"We're heading up to the second site, Zeke. There's a cave there. We think that's where Paige and Paul are."

"And how long have you known this?"

Andrew shook his head. "Back off, Zeke. We didn't have any idea of this until a while ago. One of the men mentioned it."

Zeke stared in anger at the path. "Then, what are we waiting for?"

"We can't go rushing in and you know that. We don't know how many men are

there, or even if Paige and Paul are there.
Even if they were, they could well have
been moved.”

“And they could be dead, too, now
couldn’t they?”

Andrew watched as Zeke walked
away, kicking at stones as he went. His
heart raised in prayer for him and Paige,
Andrew turned as Tad and Don approached.

“How do you want to do this,
Andrew?”

“We’ll head up to the site, Tad. With
this rain, we’re not likely to pick up a scent
trail for Beauty, are we?”

Tad shrugged. “Not likely. I’ll get
Suzy and Beauty. Lead off when you’re
ready.”

Andrew pulled out his phone and
checked the message that had come in. His
heart sinking, he shoved the phone back into
his pocket. Brown was still on the loose.
Just what he needed.

Forty-five minutes later, Andrew
stopped his group with an upraised hand.
The rain had lessened to a degree and he
could see across the clearing. He pointed

for the men to separate and head towards the far side of the clearing. His hand stopped Zeke from moving forward.

"You're a civilian here, Zeke. Stay behind me, or I'll assign someone to take you back to the vehicles. Got it?" Andrew's voice sounded harsher than he meant it to, but he knew Zeke would not stay back unless he was extra firm with him.

Zeke finally nodded, dropping back behind Andrew as he made his way forward. Listening intently, Andrew and Tad headed into the cave, flashlights in hand. Empty! Andrew shook his head. They had to be here but weren't. Tad went back for Suzy and Beauty, handing Suzy the bag with a scarf of Paige's in it. Beauty sniffed, then headed into the cave, alerting to where Paige had been sitting.

"They were here, Zeke. I have no idea where they are now." Suzy turned to the entrance. "We'll have to rely on ourselves to search unless Beauty can pick up a scent of some kind."

Commotion outside the cave had Andrew running that way. He slid to a stop as he watched Don pick a man up from the ground.

"Brown! What a surprise! Come to finish the job?"

Brown tried to rub the mud off his clothes. "I have no idea what you're talking about."

Andrew snorted. "Sure you do. By the way, you're under arrest. The list is long. Cuff him and head back to the station with him." He pointed to two of the officers.

"Now, Suzy, what do you suggest?"

"I suggest we break up into teams of two and each take an area to search. There are lots of game trails up this way. Keep in contact with one another. We'll regroup in an hour at the vehicles. All the trails lead back that way." She watched as most of the men moved off, except for Don, Zeke, Tad and Andrew.

She paced, something niggling at the back of her mind. Tad watched, finally speaking.

"What's got you bothered, Suzy?"

"I don't know, Tad. Beauty says they were here, but how long ago and where are they now?"

"Are there any cabins or shelters in the area?" Zeke spoke up, as he eyed the skin. Morning light was coming and the storms were moving off, rain lessening as they did so.

Tad went to shake his head, then spun, his eyes narrowed as he searched the area.

"Suzy, where was that cabin we stumbled on a few years ago? Wasn't it near here somewhere?"

"That's what it was, Tad. The cabin." Suzy turned in a circle, her eyes searching the forest before finally pointing. "That way. It's about two hours from here, if I remember correctly. But it was in really bad shape when we found it, what five years ago?"

"That would be about right."

Andrew stared at the two, then pointed. "Lead the way, Tad. Let's get a move on and pray that's where they are."

Chapter 24

$\mathscr{P}$aul pulled the door to the cabin open and stepped out, looking up at the sky and then around. The rain had stopped. Time to get underway. He hoped Shane knew where he was and how to get out of there.

Shane stepped out behind him. "We'll be able to get back to one of the parking lots now. If we head to the west when we head out, that will take us to where I have a truck hidden."

"Planning ahead?"

Shane shrugged. "Given my life, I'm always prepared." He turned to look back at the cabin. "Is she going to be able to walk?"

Paul sighed. "I really don't know, Shane. She's not responding at all to me. I'll try to rouse her."

Paul crouched down by Paige and studied her face. She had finally closed her eyes, but he couldn't be certain that she had even slept. Hand on her shoulder, he gently shook her.

"Paige, come on. Let's get you on your feet."

Paige roused, her eyes slowly opening, but still not focusing on him. He pulled her to her feet and grasped her hand to pull her with him.

"Come on, Paige. We've got quite a walk ahead of us. We need to get on our way."

Paige let Paul pull her to her feet, tripping slightly as she moved forward. She couldn't concentrate. Her mind felt like it was in a fog. What was wrong with her, she wondered, then shuddered. When would Brown catch up with them? Would she ever see Zeke or her family again? Lord, I can't even pray anymore. Help me.

Shane shot a look at Paige, then at Paul. "We'll likely end up carrying her at some point. She's sick."

Paul nodded, then scooped Paige up into his arms. "Lead the way. If we make stops, we should be okay. How long a walk?"

Shane shrugged. "By myself, maybe three hours. With Paige like she is, more likely four to five."

Paul nodded, his eyes searching the area around them. "Let's go then."

Four hours later, Shane held up his hand and pointed towards the parking lot ahead of them.

"Let me check it out first." He pointed off to the side. "There's some shelter in there. Hide there. I'll be back."

Paul pulled Paige in with him. She had finally insisted that she walk, although she had stumbled many times. He watched as she sank to the ground, her energy spent. His eyes in constant movement, he listened for Shane to return.

Hearing soft footsteps, he turned, ready to attack who was coming. Shane peeked in and then motioned Paul to come out.

"We're safe, so far. But we need to make plans. Where will I drop you two off? I can't be seen doing that."

By this time, Paul had figured out that Shane was undercover. He just wasn't sure what force he was on.

"Let me think for a moment." Paul turned to watch Paige, his thought processes foggy with fatigue. He paced, not wanting to ask Paige.

"Paige?" He waited until she looked up at him. Her face was white and drawn and he could hear a rasp in her breathing. He needed to get her to medical care. "Where can Shane drop us off where he can't be seen?"

Paige tried to focus, finally speaking. "If he drops us off near the library, that should be okay. I don't think there are any cameras there and we can get help." She coughed, her body rocking with it.

Paul scooped her up again, concern coursing through him at the heat he could feel coming from her.

"Shane, we need to get her to the hospital now."

Shane nodded. "Then, let's go. I don't want to stay out here too long. I don't want Brown catching us."

"Do you think he's after us?"

"Yep. He'll keep after us until he dies, if he can. He's a sore loser."

Paul tucked Paige into the truck, fastening her seatbelt, then climbing in beside her.

Shane drove away, eyes watchful. He couldn't feel any eyes on them, but he couldn't be sure. He drove directly to the hospital, waited until Paul had pulled Paige from the truck and headed inside, then drove away, eyes still watchful. He was heading for Oak City and his contact there. He needed to know what was happening.

❂ ❂ ❂ ❂

Zeke stood at the doorway of the cabin and looked around. Beauty had alerted to Paige being there. But she wasn't. Where was she?

Don laid a hand on his shoulder. "It looks as if Paul is walking out with her, Zeke."

"It does, but he's not alone. So is he walking out as a free man or as a captive?"

"I would say a free man." Andrew walked towards him. "Suzy says Beauty is alerting to the left. We'll go that way. Tad says this leads to another parking lot I didn't know about. I've called in the other men and they'll meet us there."

Zeke nodded, then turned to walk away, his thoughts mixed. Where is she, Lord? Is she okay? I can't bear the thought of losing her. She'll take a huge chunk of my heart if I do.

Andrew and Don watched Zeke as he paced.

"He's hurting, Andrew."

"I know. We need to get him and Paige back together. His friends have set up a prayer chain and are waiting for me to call them in to help search. I pray we don't get to that point."

Don nodded. "I somehow don't think we will. Suzy's ready to move off."

Three hours later, they emerged from the forest, not having found Paige or Paul, but Beauty leading them forward as fast as she could.

Andrew pulled out his phone as it chimed. As he listened, his eyes sought Zeke's. Don watched his face, then nodded.

As Andrew closed his phone he turned and paced before heading for Zeke. He stopped for a quiet word with Don.

"Zeke? Let's go."

"Just like that, we're leaving?"

"Yes. Now get into the vehicle." Andrew waited for the anger to emerge he knew Zeke had building in him, then watched as Zeke just turned and walked to the vehicle, slamming the door behind him.

"Andrew?" Don's quiet voice came from beside him. "You have news?"

"I do. Paul's been in touch with Bill. They're at the hospital. He's okay, but Paige is sick. The physician's assessing her now."

"How did they get away?" Don's voice held a question.

"Apparently one of the gang was an undercover officer of some kind. He got them away, dropped them off at the hospital, and took off. He had planned for this."

Don shook his head. "A miracle if you ask me. How did God put someone in the very spot they were needed?"

"That's where faith comes in, Don, faith and trust. Let's go."

Zeke's anxiety mounted more and more as he watched the direction they were headed.

"Andrew.   What aren't you telling me?"

Andrew sighed to himself. He had to tell him and he wasn't quite sure how. "Paul and Paige are safe, Zeke. I don't know all the details yet.   Paul's okay, but Paige is sick."

"Sick? With what?"

"I have no idea, Zeke. You'll find out when I get you to the hospital?" Andrew bit back the frustration he was feeling. There were a lot of loose ends to tie up and he was tired to the point his bones felt like each one was aching.

Zeke was out of the vehicle and into the Emergency Department almost before Andrew had stopped the vehicle, Don on his heels.

Zeke stopped at the registration desk, anxiety flying off him. The clerk looked up and then frowned.

"My wife? She was brought in. Paige Benson?"

The clerk checked her patient list, then pointed at the waiting room.

"I'll let the physician know you're here. You can't go back yet. They're treating her."

Zeke bit back anger and words as he watched her walk towards the treatment area, then turned himself towards the waiting room. He paced, Don standing watching him. Andrew, after a quick word with Don, had left. Don searched for Paul, not seeing him, and he hesitated before he went to have a quiet word with the clerk. He nodded, then took his stand once more where he could see as much as possible.

Zeke turned as he heard footsteps approaching him and frowned. He didn't know this man, did he? He shook his head as the man stopped in front of him, Don moving closer to him.

"Ezekiel Benson?" The man didn't wait for Zeke to respond. "I'm Nathaniel George. I've been following your work for years now. I'd like to talk with you about a job offer when the time's right. Here's my card."

Zeke stared at the piece of paper in his hand as the man walked away. Don took the card from him and pocketed it.

"I'll check him out for you, Zeke. Right now, you have more important things to worry about." Don nodded towards the exam rooms. "I think that's the physician you're wanting to speak to.:

Zeke turned, heart in his mouth at the grim look on the physician's face.

"Zeke? I'm Dr. Peters. I've been treating your wife, Paige. Come with me. I'll take you to her." Don followed behind them, eyes alert, as the physician shot him a quick look. "First, she's alive. Battered a bit from what's she been through. Bruising from rough treatment. But she's sick, Zeke and we can't determine the exact cause. It's like she has pneumonia and we're trying to come up with an antibiotic she can use. Every one we test doesn't work."

Zeke stopped, his face paling. "What aren't you saying, Dr. Peters?"

"We've put her on a ventilator, Zeke, to help her breath. We're working through a combination of drugs now. It's like it's a chemical that caused the pneumonia."

Zeke turned to Don as he spoke. "Her hands were burnt a few days ago by a chemical. Test that. I'm sure you still have some of that around. If not, talk to Andrew at the police department. He'll know the chemical you want."

The physician shook his head. "I really don't want to know what this is all about, but your wife is sick. Don, is it? Your man's okay, just soaked through. He's next door."

Don shook his head. "I don't leave Zeke or Paige. They're under my protection."

The physician threw up his hands. "Of course, they are." He pointed at the curtain. "Behind there. I'll be back in a few minutes."

Chapter 25

Zeke hesitated, hand on the curtain, a prayer on his lips before he pulled the curtain back and stopped, his eyes on Paige. She lay still, her face whiter it seemed that the pillow she was laying on. His ears took in the beeping and hiss of the equipment, his eyes tracing the lines and tubes running from them to Paige.

Oh, Paige! What did we get into, sweetheart? Stopping by the bedside, his hand reached for her face, resting on her forehead. His eyes slid shut and he shuddered, hearing faintly the rasp of her breathing under the sounds of the ventilator breathing for her.

Don stood just inside the curtain, arms folded across his chest, prayers going up. He shook his head. It didn't look good, he thought. If they can't trace the chemical, they can't treat her. A movement outside the curtain had him stepping backwards and meeting Paul's eyes.

"Paul? You okay?"

"A headache and some bruised ribs added to the soaking we got. How's Paige?"

Don hesitated, then spoke. "She has pneumonia, Paul, they think from a chemical exposure."

"Chemical? That explains it then."

"Explains what?"

"You didn't notice? She hasn't felt well for a few days. I noticed it but just thought it was the stress they were under and the pain from her hands."

Don sighed. "I guess after all it wasn't. Now what, Paul? You need to get some dry clothes."

"Thomas is on his way in with some for myself and Zeke. Andrew stopped briefly to see him. Bill's coming back to get my statement." He spun in a circle, staring around. "Did they catch everyone?"

"I have no idea, but for some reason, I don't think they did. Did your friend say anything?"

Paul shook his head. "He didn't say much at all, frankly. He was heading to Oak City he did say."

Don nodded, then pointed at the curtain. "I'll stay with them for now. You wait out there for Thomas. Do you need to leave?"

Paul stared at him. "Are you kidding? Not a chance, Don. Not until all of them are caught."

"About what I figured you said. Do you have money to get a hot drink and some food?"

Paul nodded. "I do. They didn't bother to search very well."

Don gave a small laugh. "Didn't get all your weapons?"

Paul shook his head. "Say, did they find a younger man in the cave?"

"No. Should they have?"

"They should have. I suspect he's long gone from here. He wasn't a happy camper at all."

Zeke vaguely heard Don and Paul talking, his eyes on Paige. He traced her chin with his finger, missing the tape that held the ventilator in place. Would they be able to find a treatment option? He prayed they did. He couldn't handle losing her.

He stirred as he heard movement at the curtain and then Paige's Mom was beside him, tears on her cheek as she reached to touch her daughter's face. Zeke wrapped an arm around her and then around Meg on his other side. Paige's Dad stood, a grim look on his face.

"Who did this, Zeke?"

"I don't have those answers. You need to talk to Bill or Andrew."

"And I will be."

Late that night, Zeke sat, eyes once more on Paige, watching as she struggled to breathe. The physician who admitted her had told him they were working on a treatment plan but still hadn't totally found one. His hand reached to grasp hers, tightening around it as if he could drag her back and help her breathe.

The sound of the door opening and swishing closed and quiet footsteps reached his ears. He looked up through blurry eyes. Bill stood there, his gaze on Page.

"Bill?"

"How is she, Zeke?"

He shrugged. "About what you'd expect. They're trying to come up with a treatment."

Bill sighed. "I just gave her doctor some more information. Gary Brown has talked. Hopefully, this will let them treat her." He didn't add that the physician had told him she only had a few more hours and they wouldn't be able to save her.

Zeke stared at him, the words not meaning anything for a moment. "Will it be enough and in time?"

"He thought it would. How are you?"

Zeke just shot him a glare, then turned his eyes back to Paige, not saying anything.

Bill stood for a few minutes, then spoke. "Listen. Your friends are gathered in the waiting room. They plan on staying all night. Noah's started up the prayer chain at the church."

Zeke sat, not saying anything. "Is it enough, Bill? Will He hear and answer?"

"He will, Zeke, but you may not like what His answer is. I pray for peace for you, no matter how it comes out. We need to talk tomorrow." He hesitated, then walked away.

❋ ❋ ❋ ❋

Two days later, Paige stirred, her eyes fluttering open and closed. She couldn't keep them open, no matter how much she wanted to. She sighed softly, slipping back into that darkness, the darkness that kept calling her name, drawing her deeper and deeper into it.

Zeke bent over her, hand on her forehead, softly calling her name. He watched as she sank back into that blackness, his heart sore. She had been awake. Would she wake again? The physician had finally found a treatment but had told Zeke it might not work, given how deep the pneumonia had a hold on her. Zeke had stared him down, telling him God was in control. The physician had shrugged and walked away, waving a hand in dismissal.

Zeke turned as the door swung open and Josiah and Faith stood there. They hesitated and then approached him.

"Zeke?" Faith's voice was quiet, the question unsure.

"She was just awake, Faith, but she didn't stay with me." The tears he could no longer control trickled down his face and he swiped angrily at them.

Faith's arm swept around him and he heard her quiet prayer. A sense of peace finally flooded him. He reached to hug Faith, his eyes on Josiah.

"Thank you, you two."

Josiah nodded. "Listen, we won't stay. We'll be in the waiting room. Noah's still heading up the prayer chain. It's going round the clock."

"Thank him for me, please?"

Zeke finally sank into the chair the nurses had provided. They had learned he would not leave Paige's side, not even when they gave a treatment. His eyes shut and he slept.

Paige's eyes fluttered open once more, this time staying open. She stared around her, trying to figure out just where she was. She turned her head enough to look at the monitors and then to the ventilator. She traced the lines and tubing running to her body. She was safe. How? She felt a moment of fear. Zeke? Where was he? Then she realized someone had her hand in his. Her head turned and her face softened as she saw Zeke, slumped in a chair, a blanket covering him, her hand snug in his. She squeezed his, but he slept. Her face turned to his, she slept as well.

The physician stared at Paige the next morning, then at her chart, a look of disbelief on his face.

"You shouldn't be awake, Paige. In fact, you should be dead. That chemical was brutal."

Zeke gave a laugh. "You doubted me, Doctor. You now see the proof."

"Yeah, I guess I do. Paige, we're going to keep you on the ventilator for a while longer, just to let your lungs heal more. It was more than just pneumonia. That came from the soaking and fatigue and whatever else you've been through. Our guess is that when you touched that stone, somehow you breathed in just enough of the chemical to damage the lungs. They'll heal but it will take time." He turned to walk away, his feet stopping until he shook his head and walked away.

Paige and Zeke exchanged a glance, then Zeke gathered her close.

"It's over, sweetheart. Andrew tells me they've arrested the leader of it all. He'll be by in a day or so just to give us an update on the investigation and charges. He says it's been a dirty piece of work, to quote him."

Paige nodded as her eyes slid shut. Zeke watched her face as it relaxed, his heart thankful she was still with him.

❂ ❂ ❂ ❂

Bill finally caught up with Zeke and Paige four days later. Paige was snuggled into Zeke's arms where they sat on a couch in her hospital room. Bill sank into a chair near them, his eyes sliding closed for a moment. The investigation had taken a lot from him, a lot of hours worked that he didn't wish on anyone else.

"Bill?" Paige's voice was still hoarse.

"Paige? Zeke? You two doing okay now?"

Zeke stared down at Paige's head. "Yeah, we are. Paige is going home tomorrow. And I have a new position right here in town."

"That's great. Now about the investigation."

"We've been waiting for an update. So, tell us."

"Okay." He sat back, rubbing his hands. "It's hard to know when to start. And don't tell me the beginning is where to start. Because this story has more than one beginning." He sighed. "Paige, what do you remember about Gary's father?"

"Not a lot. I never liked or trusted him. He had a cruel streak a mile wide. I always wondered if his wife was a battered woman. Gary certainly had the stigmata of a battered child."

"He did and he was. He lashed out at his father years ago and then left home. He hasn't seen his parents since them. The accident that put his mom in a wheelchair? His dad did that. All this has been leading

277

up to where he ended up. He saw a chance to make a lot of money and flash it in his father's face. Little did he know he was working for a crook."

"Who was the head of it all?" Zeke shared a look with Paige. "Paige maintains that Gary didn't have the brains to plan out something like this, chemist or no."

"No, he didn't. He came up with the chemical. The plan was to threaten to release it and destroy forests in its path. All to take over a paper and pulp mill."

Zeke stared at him. "But they don't make a lot of money anymore."

Bill nodded. "No they don't but they planned to change that. I don't have all the particulars, those are sealed for court, but the person in charge had tried this elsewhere with something different and it worked. They didn't really care if people got sick or died. They were collateral damage."

"Collateral damage?" Paige's voice held anger, then resignation. "Who was the leader, Bill?"

Bill stared at her for a while, then shook his head. "Not who we expected, Paige. Les Major."

"Les? What? Why? He's been in business here since we were kids. He's even been on town council. Wasn't running the newspaper enough for him?"

"Newspaper? Don't tell me. He owned the newspaper?" Zeke was dumbfounded.

Bill nodded at Zeke's question. "He did. He hasn't said why he wanted the pulp mill. That's something we'll not likely know now."

"What do you mean? Not know? Isn't he talking?" Paige stared at Bill.

Bill shook his head. "He had a heart attack, Paige, when we went to arrest him. He didn't make it. No justice there for you. The team is working through all the paperwork he's accumulated over the years, and it's a lot. And that tracking device? He slipped it to you at the conference, needing to know where you were at all times."

Paige sat back, Zeke's arm tight around her. "No justice for us, but he'll face a higher Judge.   Thanks for telling us. Everyone else involved has been arrested?" At Bill's nod, she continued, "Then I can go home not having to look over my shoulder." She stopped, a puzzled look on her face. "The man that led Paul and I to safety. Who was he? I know Paul came to trust him. I was too out of it to know what was going on."

Bill and Zeke shared a glance. "He was undercover, trying to get evidence. I have no idea what force or organization he worked for. Listen. I have to run. If you two need anything, let me know."

Zeke held his wife close waiting for her to speak.

"God watched out for us, didn't he, Zeke? You said He would but I had my doubts. Through it all, I've finally found that peace you talked about. I'm eager to get home and back to work."

"I know you are but you'll not be working for a few weeks. You need to heal."

"I know." Her disgruntled comment caused him to laugh, bringing her face back so she could stare at him.

He captured her lips with his, the kiss sweet with promise and love. "You'll heal, we'll make plans, and live the life God has chosen for us. I love you so much. When I thought I had lost you, I didn't know how I would go on."

She nodded. "I know. Zeke, we need to do more than just live our lives. We need to reach out in some way." She settled back, her thoughts already on the future.

Epilogue

Three months later, Zeke went looking for his wife at her office, a bouquet of yellow roses in his hand. Meg laughed at him, then pointed toward the chart room. He peeked in. Paige was hard at work, her back to the door. He cleared his throat, the bouquet in front on him.

Paige spun, a smile lighting up her face. "Zeke. Are those for me? Thank you." She reached up to kiss him. "What are you doing here in the middle of the afternoon?"

"Just came to visit my wife?" When she shook her head, a smile on her face, he grinned. "I'm being sent to the capitol and was told you can come with me. I have to do some research there for the project we're working on."

"Research, is it?" She pretended to think about it. "All right. You've twisted by arm. When do you have to go?"

"Tonight. We can fly in and be there in time for a late dinner. I've packed your prettiest clothes."

"Zeke!" She reached to hug him, her flowers in hand. "But what about my work?"

"Meg says you don't have any clients booked for the next two days. We'll be back by the weekend. We need to get away and this is the perfect opportunity."

She leaned back to look up at him. "You're right. We do need to get away, to get a fresh perspective on life. Have I told you today that I love you?"

He nodded. "I never tire of that. I love you so much too, sweetheart. Well, ready to run away with me?"

She laughed again, grabbed her purse and briefcase, and handed Meg the roses on the way by. Meg shook her head at the two before burying her nose into the roses. Her prayer was that she found someone just as special for herself.

Dear Readers:

Thank you for choosing to read the story of Zeke and Paige. Weather - no matter where you live, you face all kinds of weather. Maps - we no longer use the paper ones, depending instead on the internet or GPS.

I have always been fascinated with maps. As a child, I would pull out the provincial map and study it, tracing paths I would want to travel. As an adult, my Sheltie and I would take off, not knowing what road we were on, just that we were headed in the right direction. And my Dad would have had a fit if he had seen some of the roads Hamish and I traveled.

My Dad was a merchant mariner in WWII and in the RCN in the Korean war. I loved to talk with him about the weather. Some of my more vivid memories are standing with him, watching the clouds roll in and seeing the lightning, hearing him describe it, some based on his sea travels, most based on what he had observed over the years. Even the last year he was alive, we would stand at the window and watch the lightning or the snow storms moving in.

Now, the tornado. I always knew one would pop up somewhere along the line. I went through the Barrie, Ontario, one in 1985, being right on the edge of it. Scary stuff and not something I would ever want to repeat. Tornadoes are part of nature and there's not a lot we can do. Thankfully, since 1985, the warnings are getting out in the Province of Ontario where I live.

Peace - How much we long to have peace in this day and age. The world is full of sorrow, trouble, and wars. But we can still have the peace that God gives. It's there for the asking. And He has promised His peace is not as the world would give us.

Thank you once more for sharing in the story of one of His Warriors. And I know - Ian and Joseph from His Guardians just had to show up, didn't they? I miss those guys. And Don - he was in Abe's story in His Guardians. Now, I would ask you, does he and his team deserve their own stories? Stay tuned on that one.

God bless each one of you.

Ronna